R.

CARA MALONE

LISBON PRESS

CHAPTER ONE

*E*d Wallace drove along a dark and neglected two-lane road south of Fox City, swerving periodically to avoid potholes and gritting his teeth whenever he thought of his wife.

"No, *you* let the GD cat out," he grumbled to himself. "Always opening the front door just to talk to the stupid neighbor."

The neighbor in question, James, lived across the street. He was five years younger than Ed, had all of his hair, and never seemed to actually go inside his damn house. Ed had wondered on more than one occasion if his wife was actually sleeping with James, or just wished she was.

In any case, someone left the door open after dinner tonight and the cat got out. Ed and his wife had discovered that fact about eleven o'clock, just before bed, because Nadine preferred to spoon with the friggin' cat rather than her own husband, and lo and behold, the furball was missing in action.

It was Ed's fault, just like everything else that went wrong in Nadine's charmed world, and a fight had ensued. When she was done screeching at him, Nadine put on her ratty old bathrobe—probably never wore *that* when she thought James might see her—and went outside with a flashlight to look for the cat.

Rather than spend the next few hours looking for a black cat in the dark before lying down next to an ice-cold wife for the night, Ed had grabbed a six-pack out of the garage refrigerator and took off. He was out of the neighborhood before he even had a destination in mind, and at that hour, there was only one place to go.

He had a hunting cabin in the woods south of the city. Ed liked to hunt white-tailed deer, which weren't in season right now—the middle of the summer—but he had no plans to do anything other than drink and avoid the wife tonight anyway.

It was past midnight by the time he reached the potholed road that led into the woods, and his was the only vehicle for miles, or so it seemed. Still angry about the chewing out that he had *not* deserved, he kept looking sidelong at that six-pack in the passenger seat.

Just one while he was driving wouldn't hurt. He still had another twenty minutes or so on that long, straight road before he reached the turn-off for his cabin, and it wasn't like there were any witnesses around.

Definitely no cops in this rural area so late at night.

Just as Ed was plucking a can out of the plastic ring,

he saw some light up ahead on the road. He dropped the beer can into the cupholder beside him and mumbled, "What's all that?"

The light was unsteady and his first guilty thought was that there *was* a copper out here after all, just lying in wait for some unlucky bastard like Ed to come by. Hell, the cop's name would probably end up being James, too.

But the closer Ed got, he could tell that was no police light bar, or even a dome light. As he got closer, he realized it was a fire.

Way the hell out here, in the middle of nowhere.

"What the hell?"

After about half a mile, Ed reached the source and his eyes went wide as he took in the sight of an SUV entirely engulfed in flames on the side of the road. He pulled over and got out of his truck, but he couldn't get within twenty feet of the burning vehicle. The heat coming off it was like a bellowing furnace.

Then Ed remembered all the action movies he'd ever seen, with gas tanks exploding and shrapnel flying, and he beat a hasty retreat.

He got back into his truck and backed a safe distance away, then reached over the beer—thank God he hadn't drunk any yet—to retrieve his cell and call 911.

His wife wasn't gonna believe this. Leave the house a cat-losing bastard, come home a hero who may well have kept the whole damn forest from catching fire. Take that, Nadine.

"*A*ll I'm saying is that I think you'd make a great detective."

Melissa Pine rolled her eyes. "Zara, you've been saying that for over a year. I hear you."

"And yet you stubbornly continue to patrol," her best friend shot back.

Mel was sitting on a loveseat in Zara's apartment, sipping on a cup of coffee while Zara and her girlfriend, Kelsey, cuddled on the couch across from her. The two of them were drinking red wine and winding down for the night, but Mel's third-shift patrol began in about an hour. Her night was just beginning.

"What can I say?" She shrugged. "I like patrol. There's nothing wrong with that."

She'd been insisting as much ever since Zara, her former partner, took the detective test and transferred to the narcotics department. It had been Zara's goal ever since she joined the force and Mel was happy for her... but it just wasn't *her* goal.

"Does it ever scare you?" Kelsey asked. "Patrolling all by yourself?"

"I mean, the job can be scary whether you're working solo or with a partner," Mel said. "Anyway, the chief gave me the option to find a new partner but I can't imagine trusting anyone else to have my back like Zara did."

"Aww," Kelsey said. "That's cute."

Mel rolled her eyes again, playfully though. Zara and Kelsey had been practically joined at the hip ever since they worked a homicide case together the previous year, and even though it sometimes felt like Mel had been replaced, there was—miraculously—no jealousy.

At least once a week, the three of them got dinner together, went out for an evening round of disc golf, or just hung out like they were doing now. In some ways it felt like Mel had gained a new best friend in Kelsey instead of losing her patrol partner.

Speaking of which... she glanced at the time on her phone. "It's getting late. I better get down to the station."

"Well, be careful out there," Kelsey warned her as she got up to take Mel's coffee cup. "We worry about you."

"Hey, my job's not nearly as dangerous as Miss Under-cover Narc's," Mel pointed out, and Kelsey frowned.

"Don't remind me."

In the six months that Zara had been a full-fledged narcotics detective, she'd gone undercover twice and been rewarded both times with successful busts. She was tearing it up in her new job, but Mel knew how much Kelsey worried about her.

"Sorry," she said. Then, by way of further apology, she added, "I'll be safe tonight. I always am."

"Think about that detective test," Zara said once again, and Mel scowled at her.

"I think your girlfriend is broken," she told Kelsey. "She just keeps saying the same thing over and over."

Kelsey smiled and wrapped her arms around Zara's waist. "Yeah, but she generally knows what she's talking about. She got me to reconsider medical school, after all."

"Yeah, but that's something you already wanted," Mel pointed out.

Kelsey had been on track to become a doctor when life took her in a different direction and she'd ended up a forensic investigator for the coroner's office. Now, she was re-enrolled in medical school, planning to become a pathologist, and just waiting for the fall semester to begin.

"Besides," Mel said, "I don't have time to study and train all over again."

Zara gave her an incredulous look. "You're single, you live alone, and you work third shift. You have all the time in the world."

"Oh, gee thanks for the reminder," Mel said.

Zara laughed. "Sorry. Didn't mean it that way."

"Yeah, it's fine," Mel said. "I know what you meant."

They'd been partners for five years before Zara made detective, and one of the nice things about getting into life-and-death situations with somebody was that minor offenses tended to roll right off your back. Zara could say just about anything to Mel and know she'd take it knowing it was said with the best intentions.

So why was Mel having such a hard time reciprocating lately?

Maybe it was because of Kelsey. As much as Mel loved her, Kelsey's very presence created distance between her and Zara. And that was okay—it was the natural order of things when your best friend fell in love. Still, it was an adjustment.

"Thanks for the coffee," she said, hugging them both in turn and seeing herself out of the apartment.

It was a short drive over to the police station, where she'd clock in and trade her little Toyota for a squad car to begin the night's patrol. While she drove, she couldn't help lingering on the fact that she used to be able to say anything to Zara, and often *did*. When you spend eight hours a night in a car with someone, you tend to dig down into the nitty, gritty depths of each other's lives.

But things had changed between them, and Mel could feel things changing inside herself as well. She felt her heart hardening and her muscles becoming tense—out of necessity to protect herself on the job as much as in her personal life.

About two miles from the station, Mel picked up her phone and dialed her grandmother's number from memory. It was past eleven o'clock at night, but Mel knew her nonna would answer—and that she'd worry if Mel didn't call before her shift started.

"Hey, baby girl," her grandmother answered after a

couple of rings. Her voice was scratchy and it sounded weaker than it had the previous night.

"Hi, Nonna," Mel said, trying not to let any of her worries leach into her voice. "How are you feeling tonight?"

"Don't you worry about me," Nonna said, which instantly made Mel frown.

If she'd been feeling good, she would have said so. *Don't worry about me* meant things weren't going so well, and it had become a fairly standard answer over the last few months. Mel's grandmother had ovarian cancer, a fact that Mel hadn't brought herself to admit to anyone else for fear that it would grow to consume every aspect of her life.

Despite her advanced age, Nonna was fighting with everything she had. The chemotherapy had been fighting back pretty hard, though.

"Is Amanda there?" Mel asked. "Is she keeping you hydrated, making sure you're eating—"

"Of course she is," Nonna interrupted, seventy-two years old and sick but still spunky enough to get impatient when people worried over her. "That's what we pay her for, isn't it?"

"Just checking," Mel said. Amanda was one of three in-home care nurses that Mel and Nonna had pooled their resources to hire when Nonna refused to move into an assisted living facility for the duration of her chemo treatment. Those nurses went a long way toward giving Mel peace of mind, but still... "I'm going to stop by in the morning when I get off work, okay?"

"Sure, sweetie," she said. "You know I'll be here."

"I'm pulling up to the police station now," Mel said, struggling to keep the emotion out of her voice as she pictured her grandmother—once a strong woman that Mel imagined was capable of anything—practically housebound and subject to the whims of nurses and the chemo drugs. "Have a good night, Nonna. I love you."

"I love you too, baby girl," Nonna said. "Be safe."

"I will," Mel promised, then ended the call.

The police parking deck was practically deserted at this time of night, and she pulled into the first parking spot she found. Then she turned the car off and closed her eyes, taking a few deep breaths while she pushed all her thoughts and emotions about Nonna's condition into the back of her mind.

She'd been performing this compartmentalization ritual before each shift for months now. Being a cop was all about being fully present in whatever situation you found yourself in—anything less than total attention was dangerous.

As Mel got out of her car, she snorted at the idea of taking the detective test. As if she could find room for anything else on her plate right now.

CHAPTER THREE

COURT

*C*ourtney Wilson had one eye on the clock and the other on her meal. It was past eleven—pretty late for dinner according to most people's schedules, but it had been her version of normal for the last few years.

She worked the midnight to eight a.m. shift as a police dispatcher, and the last thing she did every night before reporting for duty was eat dinner with her dad.

Well, she ate dinner. He usually had a bowl of ice cream or a piece of pie before bed. Tonight it was butterscotch ripple and a cup of decaf coffee—a combination that made Court's teeth hurt just watching him eat it.

"I saw on the locker room bulletin board that civil service exams are being held again next month," she said, casually taking a bite of reheated lasagna.

"No," her dad said from the other end of the dining table.

"Dad—"

"Courtney," he shot back, adopting that terribly annoying *father knows best* tone that he'd been taking with her ever since she was a little girl. Never mind the fact that she was twenty-three now and didn't want to be a dispatcher forever. Never mind the fact that she *could* sign up for the civil service exam whether he approved or not.

"Dispatchers in Fox County make thirty-five grand a year, tops," she pointed out. "Police can make up to seventy—"

"Yeah, and they can also get shot and killed in the line of duty," her dad barked back. "Courtney, we've been over this. I don't want you working in such a dangerous field. Dispatch is close enough to the action."

"Not really," she grumbled under her breath, stuffing another bite of lasagna into her cheek.

She wasn't going to press him any more on the subject tonight, though. It was something that came up every six months or so—every time the civil service exams came around and Courtney found herself hoping that her father's attitudes had changed. They never did, though, and the most annoying part of it all was that she couldn't even call him a hypocrite.

Her dad was none other than the Chief of Police, and she couldn't count the number of dangerous, thrilling, criminal-busting stories he'd told her over the years, before he'd come off the streets and settled into his big office on the top floor of the precinct. But her mom had also been a cop and she'd died in the line of duty.

So Court never pushed too hard, but she couldn't keep herself from trying every once in a while.

Maybe someday her dad would see her as a grown adult capable of making her own decisions.

And maybe someday she'd have a job that paid enough to let her get a place of her own...

"A lot of dispatchers work third shift and take classes during the day," her dad pointed out. "I know it'd be a lot of work, but you're smart, kiddo. I'd be happy if you went to school for anything that doesn't involve the potential for gunfire."

Court smiled. She was well aware that dispatch was only a waystation for a lot of people—some of her best friends at the station had worked their way up, many of them going to the police academy during the day and dispatching at night.

But this wasn't an argument she was going to win tonight. She glanced at the clock again. Eleven-thirty.

"I better get a move on," she said, wolfing down the last couple bites of lasagna. She got up from the table and gathered her plate, as well as her dad's empty ice cream bowl. As she headed into the kitchen to put it all in the dishwasher, she called over her shoulder, "Hey, the last time I went to the grocery store, I noticed this new Greek frozen yogurt. Looked pretty good."

"That your way of telling me I'm getting fat?" her dad asked, patting his belly as she came back into the dining area.

"Not exactly," she said. "But it wouldn't kill you to cut down on the sugar a little, would it?"

Her dad was a pretty healthy fifty-year-old, and the fact that he technically had a desk but rarely ever had the time to actually sit down at it helped. But Court knew from her friends on day shift that he also had a pretty serious donut habit.

"It might," he said. "You want me to go back to cigarettes?"

"Nope," Court said. "Ideally I think neither would be best."

"Well, tell the criminals in this city to stop making my job stressful and then we'll talk," he shot back. "And don't worry about me, kiddo. It's my job to worry about you."

"Yeah, well, I took over worrying about you from Mom," she answered. "Somebody's gotta do it."

Her dad got up from the table and she gave him a hug before they went their separate ways for the night—he to his bedroom for a little late-night TV until he fell asleep, and she to the police station.

*T*he station was quiet as usual when Court arrived.

She liked to get there early and take her time getting to the dispatch office because you never knew what would be going on or who you'd run into. She'd made friends with a number of the patrol officers and detectives, and hands down, the best part about working third shift was that her dad wasn't around.

Not that Court minded spending time with him—but

the fewer people around here that knew she was the chief's daughter, the better.

She never introduced herself as Courtney Wilson, lest people pick up on the significance of her last name. Sure, plenty of them already knew—her family history was pretty well-known around the precinct, especially after her mother's passing—but those who didn't just thought of her as Court the friendly dispatcher. And she liked it that way.

Tonight, there was nothing special going on. A few second-shift patrol officers were finishing up reports at their desks, and the third shift was just getting ready to go out. Court did spot Tom Logan, one of the senior homicide detectives, tapping away at his computer. She still had ten minutes before her shift started, so she meandered over to his desk.

"Hey Tom, what's got you here so late?"

"I'm on call tonight," Tom grumbled. "Supposed to just have my cell on if anybody needs me, but one of my new trainees screwed the pooch on a case report this afternoon and it took me til nine o'clock to clean up his mess. Figured why go home when I might as well stay and get caught up on paperwork?"

Tom, in his late forties, was a confirmed bachelor—evidenced by his perpetually wrinkled wardrobe—and as much as he seemed to enjoy complaining about it, he was married to his job.

"You should at least get a nap," Court suggested. "Just in case you get called out to a scene."

A little part of her was hoping for exactly that. Tom knew that Court was Chief Wilson's daughter, but he didn't care and he also didn't mind letting her pump him for information about the cases he was assigned to. If he was on call tonight, Court knew he'd give her details about anything exciting that happened overnight.

"Yeah, maybe," Tom grunted, and Court could tell that he was already absorbed in his work again.

"Okay, well, have a good night," she said, then headed to the dispatchers' office on the second floor.

She said hi to her coworkers—there were a half-dozen of them on the night shift with her—then grabbed a cup of coffee and settled into her workstation. Sometimes the nights went slow and it felt like getting paid to sit around and wait, and on other nights it felt like everybody in the city was awake and in need of some kind of help. You never knew just what kind of night you were going to have.

"How's it going so far, Bree?" Courtney asked her nearest coworker, a girl her age who was going to college during the day to be an accountant and who pretty much always had a textbook somewhere on her desk.

Bree lifted her hand in a so-so gesture, and Court laughed and rolled her eyes.

"Thanks, so informative," she said, then put her headphones on and logged into the system.

She was officially on the clock, and her pulse gave a little flutter. Even though it wasn't the police work she really wanted to be doing, she loved this job and she loved Fox County. Anything could happen, and she wanted to be ready to handle it.

Her first few calls of the night were nothing too exciting. A car accident. A backyard bonfire that got a little out of control when some drunk idiot ran out of wood and tried to burn an old picnic table... whole.

And then, about forty-five minutes into her shift, Court got a call that had her sitting up in her chair, on full alert.

"There's a car on fire out on Route 12," a man said before she'd even gotten all the way through her initial *911, what is your emergency?* prompt. "Hoo-wee, and I do mean it is *blazing*."

"Where on Route 12 are you, sir?" Court asked.

"I don't know..." the man said, but it sounded like he was getting his bearings so she waited. Just before she was going to prompt him again, he said, "A mile or two south of the Circle K gas station, I know that. It's the only one around for about ten miles."

Court started a search on her computer, trying to figure out a good estimate of his location, and while she worked, she asked, "Is there anyone injured?"

"I don't know, ma'am," the man said. "I was just driving to my hunting cabin and I came on this huge fire. I think it could jump to the woods and then we'll have a real problem."

"Okay, I'm sending a fire truck to your location now," Court said. "Can you please stay on the line?"

"Sure, I don't have anywhere better to be," he said.

Court kept questioning the man—taking his name

and making sure he stayed out of harm's way—and in the back of her mind, a familiar little tingle began. Over the last couple years of working dispatch, she'd developed a bit of a sixth sense for which cases were going to turn out to be interesting ones, and something about this one had her senses on high alert.

CHAPTER FOUR

MEL

*M*el was cruising slowly through her assigned patrol area not long after her shift began when a call came through for her on the radio.

"Vehicle on fire at mile five of Route 12," the dispatcher said. "Fire response is en route. We need an officer to take a statement. Car 34, are you in range?"

Mel practically lunged for her radio. "Yeah, I'm about ten minutes away."

Ever since she'd opted not to be assigned a new partner when Zara left, she'd been stuck doing patrols on the outskirts of the county where the chief determined it was safer for a solo officer. Talk about dull city. Most of her nights were spent circling her route, occasionally stopping for coffee, and answering run-of-the-mill calls like late-night domestic disputes and the occasional car accident, usually involving alcohol or drugs.

A vehicle on fire was at least something different, and Mel knew the location—it was pretty remote, which was curious. Could be nothing but bad luck, a wiring issue or a carelessly flicked cigarette butt.

Could be more, though.

"Copy," the dispatcher, a female with a young-sounding voice that Mel was familiar with, said. "Let me know when you arrive."

"Will do," Mel said, ending the transmission and making a U-turn on the two-lane highway.

It was pretty easy to find the vehicle in question. Route 12 was long and straight, with woods on either side, and Mel was still a few miles away when she saw the orange flames licking the night sky. A siren in the distance told her that the fire engine was on its way too, arriving from the other direction.

Mel pulled to the side of the road behind a second vehicle, a pickup truck with a man standing on the shoulder beside it. She reached for the dashboard radio and said, "Car 34 here, I just arrived on the scene."

"Thank you, 34," the young dispatcher said. Mel had gotten to know all six of the night dispatchers' voices pretty well, although she didn't have any names or faces to match up to any of them, and sometimes that annoyed her. They were her only company at night now, after all.

But right now, she had work to do.

She stepped out of the car, grabbing a notebook from the passenger seat on her way out so she could take down the details for an incident report. "Sir?"

The man on the shoulder was already watching her approach, and she met him at the back bumper of his truck.

"I'm Officer Pine," she said. "What's your name, sir?"

"Ed Wallace," he said. "Edward, if you gotta be official."

"Is that your vehicle?" she asked, pointing toward the flaming husk up ahead. The fire truck was just pulling up, its siren cut but its lights still flashing.

"No way," Ed said. "I was just driving to my cabin out here when I came on it."

Mel took down all the details Ed could give her, which didn't amount to a whole lot, then told him he could either go back the way he'd come or stay back a safe distance while the firefighters cleared the road for him to continue on his way. Then she jogged in the direction of the fire engine, where guys were setting up a floodlight to work by and unreeling a thick nylon hose.

She didn't quite get there, though. On her way past the burning vehicle, she squinted into the bright flames and caught sight of a shape slumped over in the front seat.

"Oh shit," she called, getting as close as she dared while the heat from the fire baked the air. "Hey, we got a body in here!"

"What?" one of the firefighters shouted back.

Mel looked again, making sure she really had seen what she thought she saw, then finished running over to the fire engine. "There's a body in the front seat."

"Driver?" he asked.

"I can't tell," Mel said. "Try not to disturb the body too much so we can figure that out."

The firefighter just snorted, a *yeah right* expression

that was obvious even though he was being silhouetted by the floodlight. Then he raised a hand and called for one of his crew to turn on the water, and a powerful jet shot into the flames.

Right, Mel thought. It'd been a while since she'd reported to a fire scene, but she'd been on patrol long enough to know that firefighting was not a precision endeavor. Whatever happened to the body in the course of putting out the fire would happen, and the forensics team assigned to the case would just have to work around that fact.

She glanced toward Ed, who had—predictably— lingered at the scene to watch, and then she turned her back on him while she used the radio clipped to her shoulder to talk to her dispatcher again.

"Hey, this is Car 34 at the vehicle fire," she said. "We've got a body."

"Oh shit," the dispatcher said, then recovered herself quickly. "Sorry."

Mel couldn't help laughing. Whoever this nameless, faceless woman was, Mel had gotten a pretty good idea of her personality over their many nights working together, and she tended to speak before her mind could catch up to her. Not exactly professional, and it must have made for some interesting 911 transcripts, but it was nice to talk to someone who wasn't stiff and formal like some of the others. Someone with real emotions, who wasn't afraid to show them.

"Yeah," Mel agreed. "Can you notify the medical examiner and the homicide detective on call?"

"Affirmative," the dispatcher said. Again, she couldn't seem to help herself because she asked, "Do you suspect arson, then?"

"Just following protocol," Mel said. "The forensics team will have to figure all that out."

"Copy," the dispatcher said. "Tom Logan's on call tonight. He's at the station already so he should be there in twenty."

Mel keyed off and watched the firefighters extinguish the vehicle. Once the road was passable, she managed to convince Ed Wallace to move it along because Tom Logan wasn't a fan of lookie-loos at his crime scenes and she didn't feel like getting chewed out for letting Ed hang around.

By the time Tom showed up, trailed closely by the medical examiner's white van, the burned-up vehicle was extinguished but still steaming as water evaporated off it.

Tom and one of the night shift forensic investigators, Burt Anderson, walked up to Mel together and Tom whistled as he took in the scene.

"Damn," he said. "Not much left to investigate."

"Nope," Burt said. "Trade-in value is shot to hell, that's for sure."

Tom stifled a laugh and Mel tried not to let her jaw drop. Burt had been an investigator for decades and not much fazed him anymore—to the point where he was known for off-color, cynical remarks like that one.

"How can I help?" Mel asked, trying to move things along.

"Secure the scene," Tom instructed her. "And I'd like to see your notes on the guy who called this in."

"Sure thing," Mel said.

$\mathcal{A}$bout ninety minutes later, all the excitement was over. The fire department sent a tow truck to pick up the vehicle, and rather than risk losing any trace evidence by attempting to extract the body at the scene, Burt asked them to transport the body inside the vehicle. Once he finished his on-scene investigation, he and the tow truck driver headed back to the medical examiner's office for further investigation.

Tom checked out Mel's notes and copied down Ed Wallace's contact information for himself—just in case. The firefighters hosed down the woods and grass immediately around where the vehicle had caught fire—also just in case.

"What do you think?" Mel asked while the firefighters reeled in their hoses and Tom got ready to leave too. "Was it a homicide?"

"I'm no arson investigator," Tom said, "but I've seen my fair share of fires and I know what pattern accelerants leave. I think it's safe to say that was no engine fire."

He got tight-lipped after that—he knew better than to start speculating—and a few minutes later, they were all heading their own separate ways. Mel got back in her squad car and watched Tom pulling onto the shoulder on the other side of the road to turn around, and when his unmarked car was nothing but taillights in her rearview mirror, she reached for her radio.

"This is Car 34," she announced. "Available for assignment."

"Copy that, Car 34," a male dispatcher replied, and Mel felt a little sad that the dispatcher with the faulty mouth filter must have been on another call.

She turned around in the same spot as Tom and resumed her patrol route, heading back in the direction of the Circle K she'd passed on her way to the scene. It was past two in the morning and a nice, tall coffee would taste pretty good about now.

She could also use a restroom—one of the annoyances of being a female officer assigned to work in the outskirts of town, where there were no neat city blocks and readily available toilets.

Mel radioed that she'd be out of service for a couple minutes, went into the gas station, and came back five minutes later with a coffee in one hand and a banana from the store's meager fresh fruit selection in the other. When she came back on duty—10-8 in radio speak—the dispatcher that welcomed her back was suddenly much friendlier, and thirsty for details.

"Car 34, switch over to channel 47 please," she said, and Mel used the radio clipped to her shoulder to tune to the channel the dispatcher wanted while the usual dispatch chatter continued on her dashboard.

"Car 34 here," she said.

"Hey, can you talk?" the young dispatcher asked, excitement evident in her voice. Mel smiled.

"Yeah, I'm just getting back to my route," she said. "Quiet night except for the fire."

"So... what happened?" the girl asked.

They weren't supposed to do this. Talking on a private channel wasn't completely forbidden—sometimes it was necessary when in pursuit of a suspect you thought might be listening via a scanner, and sometimes it was just to avoid crosstalk on the main dispatch channel. Using a private channel just to feed juicy details to a curious dispatcher, though... that was frowned upon.

But sometimes the silence of solo patrol really got to Mel, particularly lately, when silence led to brooding over what was going on with her nonna.

And sometimes she just enjoyed making this particular dispatcher's night—which she clearly did any time she indulged the girl's questions.

"Tom said there was evidence of an accelerant," Mel told her now. "So it's looking likely that the fire was set intentionally."

"And the body?" the dispatcher asked. "That makes it a homicide, right?"

"Not necessarily," Mel said. This was quickly getting out of her field of expertise, but she found herself wanting to please the voice in her ear. "The car was still pretty hot even after the fire was put out, so the investigator couldn't get too close to the body. Impossible to tell until the autopsy whether the victim died in the fire or before."

"But you don't just find a dead body and set it on fire," the girl argued back. "It *must* be a homicide."

"You talk like somebody who reads too many detective novels," Mel teased. "Are you sure you're in the right job?"

The channel went quiet for a minute and Mel wondered if the dispatcher had gotten pulled back onto the main channel for a call. She waited, but nothing came over her dash radio. So then she started to wonder if she'd crossed a line teasing the woman.

She reached for her banana, and then the radio on her shoulder crackled back to life. "Definitely not," the dispatcher said. "I want to take the civil service exam. Was it hard when you took it?"

"No," Mel said. "But the police academy was no walk in the park."

"I can handle it," the dispatcher said. Mel found herself nodding along, although this girl would definitely need to learn not to jump to conclusions if she wanted to be a cop—and her instructors at the academy would immediately knock the looseness from her tongue.

She barely knew the woman, except through the radio, and yet Mel felt confident that she was right, she *could* handle the academy.

CHAPTER FIVE
COURT

*C*ourt let out a wide yawn while she waited in line at the little Quick Mart across the street from the police station. It was part café, part convenience store, and the owners knew their clientele were mainly people just getting to work or just leaving a shift at the precinct.

Court bought a yogurt parfait and a large cup of coffee and then, instead of heading for home like usual, she went back across the street and upstairs to her dad's office.

"Aha," she said as she pulled the door open unannounced, interrupting him as he raised a jelly donut to his mouth. "Caught you."

He gave her a grunt and set the donut down. "Aren't you supposed to be going home to sleep?"

"Good to see you too, Dad," she said, picking up his donut and setting down the yogurt parfait in its place.

She knew he'd probably go right back to the donut box in the break room after she left, but a girl could try. "Eat that—still sweet, but good for you."

"Thank you, kiddo," he said, without actually sounding all that happy about the yogurt. "Did you come all the way up here just to make sure I eat right?"

Not exactly, she thought. She had an ulterior motive for sticking around this morning, but just like she didn't want too many people around here knowing she was the chief's daughter, she also didn't want her dad knowing what she was up to today.

"Yeah, I'm not tired just yet," she lied. "Figured I'd come say hi before I went home."

"That coffee for me too?" he asked, eyeing the cup in her hand.

Damn it—here goes lie number two for the day. That was a lot for so early in the morning, and she hated being dishonest, especially with her father and only living parent.

"Nah," she said, "this is decaf for me. I would have brought you a cup but you know how the Quick Mart is at shift changes. They were all out of regular and I'd have had to stand around for five minutes waiting for them to brew more."

"That's okay, kiddo, I'm sure there's coffee in the break room," her dad said. "Thanks for the yogurt."

Court laughed. "That was the most grudging thanks I've ever heard."

"And I suppose you're going to eat that donut yourself?" he asked. "What kind of father would I be if I let you take a sugar rush for me?"

He reached for it, but Court held the plate out of his reach. "Don't worry, I'll find a good home for it."

His phone rang, and thus another busy day began for the chief of police. Court waved goodbye and her dad mouthed *goodbye* back to her before picking up the phone. Court checked the time—about twenty after eight —and decided that she'd killed enough time. She took the stairs to the next floor down, where the homicide detectives had their desks, and found Tom Logan.

His collar looked limp and his cotton shirt was wrinkled, and he had decidedly more stubble on his chin now than he'd had at midnight. Court guessed that he'd crashed in the on-call bunk room at some point last night, and he was yawning at his desk now.

"Hey Tom," Court said cheerfully, setting down the coffee—definitely not decaf—and the donut in front of him. "Figured you could use a pick-me-up. Are you going to start investigating that arson case from last night?"

Tom gave her a sidelong look and Court knew that he had her number. You didn't get to be one of the senior homicide detectives in the department without being able to read people pretty quickly.

He narrowed his eyes at her, then glanced at the donut. "Is this a bribe? Because you know cops aren't allowed to take bribes."

Court just shrugged. "I don't see a bribe. All I see is a jelly donut and a cup of coffee."

He picked the donut up and bit into it, raspberry jelly seeping out the side. With his mouth still stuffed, he asked, "So what do you want?"

"I was hoping to hear more about the investigation," she said. "You know I don't get many details when I'm stuck in the dispatchers' office. The more I can learn now, the quicker a study I'll be once I'm in the police academy."

Tom polished off the donut in just a couple bites and said, "I thought your dad didn't want you in the academy."

She shrugged again. "I'm going to wear him down sooner or later... and in the meantime, we don't have to tell him that you're keeping me in the loop on this case."

Tom washed the donut down with a long sip of coffee. Then he gave Court an appraising look. He'd done this for her before, and even let her tag along on a witness interview here and there under the guise of job shadowing, as long as she promised to keep her mouth shut—both in front of the witness and in regard to her dad. Deep down, Court was pretty sure Tom liked living on the wild side and going against the chief's wishes now and then.

He opened his mouth, but before any words came out, a female police officer came up to his desk, asking, "Detective Logan?"

With just those two words, Court recognized her voice. It was Car 34. And damn, Car 34 was cute as hell.

She looked a few years older than Court—maybe her late twenties—and she was petite in every sense of the word, a few inches shorter than Court and thin with long, straight dark hair pulled back in a ponytail that only served to exaggerate that lean effect. She had bronze-toned skin and matching rich brown eyes, and... oh, Court was staring.

"Mel," Tom said, then looked at the clock. "Shouldn't you be out of here by now?"

"Ordinarily, yes," said Car 34—Mel, or Officer Pine, according to the metallic nameplate on her breast pocket. She looked at Court, a spark in her gaze, then asked, "Sorry, am I interrupting?"

"Nah, we're just chatting," Tom said. "This is my friend, Court."

"Hi," Court said, suddenly feeling oddly shy.

"So, what's up?" Tom asked Mel.

"I was actually wondering if you would mind my tagging along a little bit when you go out to investigate that potential homicide from last night," she said. "I know you let Zara shadow you when she was trying to make detective."

Tom arched his brows. "Ah, so she finally got to you, convinced you to follow in her footsteps?"

Mel smiled, a cute little dimple appearing on just one cheek. "Not exactly. I like being on patrol... but it does get kind of lonely at night." Court sensed there was something she wasn't saying—maybe she was wrestling with whether or not to mention the fact that she'd allowed a dispatcher to squeeze details out of her about the case? Then Mel added, "I'm just curious to see what happens

CARA MALONE

in an investigation after the responding officer is finished with it, I guess."

"And this one in particular caught your fancy?" Tom asked.

Courtney couldn't help smiling. It *did* seem kind of convenient, considering the fact that the woman she knew as Car 34 had been on the job for years now. She could have decided to shadow a case at any point, but she'd picked this one. Court wasn't exactly in a position to tease, though.

"Yeah, I suppose so," Mel said.

"Well, seems like there's a lot of that going around," Tom said, then gestured to Court. "Courtney here was just asking me the same thing."

Mel's eyes went to her again, searing into her and making her pulse flutter, and Court knew she wasn't going to get away with any more one-word answers. "Umm, yeah," she said. "I probably sound different in person, but I was dispatching that call."

Mel smiled again. There was that little dimple that made her face asymmetrically charming. Her eyes went to Court's lips while she spoke, and then she said, "You look pretty close to how I was picturing you. Funny how rarely that happens."

She'd been picturing her?

Court resisted the urge to grin, to read something into that statement, to ask Officer Mel Pine whether that meant she was pleased or disappointed with the girl standing in front of her now. Lord, when was the last time she'd had such an insta-crush on a pretty woman?

Down, Courtney, down.

She was about to say something embarrassing in response, like, *you're much hotter than I pictured.* Not that she'd been imagining an ogre driving Car 34 or anything. It was just that she fielded a lot of calls from a lot of different voices every night, and she didn't have a whole lot of time to imagine faces to go with all of them. Sometimes the voices blurred into one another... but never Car 34's.

Thankfully, Tom rescued her before she could say any of that. "Well, looks like I've got two shadows for this case. You two know the rules? Keep your eyes open and your mouths shut."

"Okay," Mel agreed.

"You got it," Court answered, still wondering just what Mel had been picturing when she thought of her. She was secretly pleased at the idea that she had thought of her at all.

"Autopsy's scheduled for mid-morning," Tom said. "You two want to ride over to the medical examiner's office with me or should we go separately?"

"Together's fine by me," Mel told him, then looked to Court. "Unless you need to get home and sleep after?"

"Nope, I'm good to go," Court readily agreed. As long as her dad was too busy to find out what she was up to, she was down for whatever aspects of the investigation Tom let her tag along for. And if Mel was going to be there too, so much the better.

"Cool," Mel said. "I should get some caffeine in my system if we're going to blow past my bedtime, though."

"Me too," Court agreed. She really should have thought of that the first time she'd gone to the Quick Mart, but then she wouldn't have had the opportunity to invite Mel to tag along with her. She suggested it, and Mel readily agreed.

"I'll take a Quick Mart coffee over the stale stuff in the break room any day," she said, then looked to Tom. "You good?"

*H*e lifted the cup Court had brought him.
"I've already been bribed, err, treated. I'm just gonna check my emails—meet me back here in thirty and we'll drive over."

They agreed, then Court walked with Mel down to the Quick Mart. A few people said hello to her as they went and she waved shyly back to them, hoping not to be given away.

"Well, you're pretty popular," Mel commented as she held the door and they went outside.

"Yeah, when you work dispatch, you get to know a lot of people," Court said. Lie number three for the day, and a rough way to start getting to know someone. But people acted different around her as soon as they found out she was the chief's daughter, and she really didn't want that to happen with Mel.

"I feel like kind of a jerk for not recognizing you right away then," Mel said with a teasing smile. "I should have."

Her smile lingered, and her eyes went briefly to

Court's lips again. *I should have?* What the hell did that mean? Court was definitely getting some vibes from this woman—she just didn't know if she was making them all up out of desire and mild sleep deprivation.

She hoped not.

CHAPTER SIX
MEL

*T*he coroner's office was busy midmorning when Mel arrived with Tom and Court. Investigators were buzzing about in the cubicle-filled room where they worked. Mel could hear the sounds of centrifuges and other equipment in the chemistry and histology labs as they walked deeper into the building, and in the morgue at the back, preparations were underway for the morning's autopsies.

"How many on the schedule today?" Tom asked the autopsy assistant, Jordan, when they walked in.

"Five," she answered, pulling a gurney out of the refrigerated room where bodies were kept. "Dr. Trace and I are going to be with you on the crispy critter, and Dr. Hanson asked me to prep this one for him."

"Two autopsies at once?" Court asked, her eyebrows rising. "Is that common?"

"It happens," Jordan said. "We've got five tables, but I've never actually seen all of them in use at once."

"Where's the... umm... decedent?" Mel asked, not wanting to repeat Jordan's *crispy critter* comment.

As far as she knew, they hadn't actually made a positive identification, although Tom had run the VIN number on the burned vehicle before they left the station. It belonged to a man named Eric Gilles, and one of today's goals was to determine whether his was the body Mel discovered at the scene.

"Still in the vehicle," Jordan said. "Ordinarily we'd want to refrigerate the remains but in this case it's just not possible until after we extract it, and Dr. Trace wanted to examine the body in situ. That's why we're doing Mr. Crispy as the first autopsy of the day. Doc'll be here in a few minutes."

Jordan kept working, moving the body on the gurney to the farthest autopsy table in the room. Meanwhile, Tom went out to the adjoining garage, where the vehicle had been dropped off by the fire department tow truck, and Mel shot a curious look at Court.

She hadn't allowed herself to look at her too much on the ride over, or even when they were at the Quick Mart getting coffee. Now that Court was right here in front of her, Mel was embarrassed at how carried away she'd allowed herself to get over the radio last night.

Just because she was lonely... just because she needed a distraction... just because Court had been easy to talk to... she'd overstepped her bounds and she knew it. And now that she knew Court in person, knew her name, knew the face that went with the voice... confusion and attraction were added to that embarrassment, combining to create a dizzying mix.

Court was young and doe-eyed, with long blonde hair and a sultry look to her gaze—at least whenever it was turned in Mel's direction. There was an undeniable attraction there, and it went both ways.

Hell, the whole reason Mel had gone to see Tom this morning was with the foolish idea of extracting more details from him as the investigation progressed, simply so she'd have a reason to talk to her mysterious dispatcher the next time they worked together. And then Court had been there. And suddenly Mel had been agreeing to forego sleep in order to shadow Tom for as much of the case as he'd allow...

It had all happened fast, and by the time Tom came back in from the garage, Mel was wondering just what it was about this girl that made her take leave of her senses so quickly and completely.

"How does it look?" Court asked.

Tom frowned. "Not good. Hope you're not squeamish."

Court shook her head, fearless, and Mel stood a little taller, wanting to appear the same. Then Jordan called from the autopsy table, "Hey, anybody want to test out their squeamishness level for real?"

Mel furrowed her brow. "What do you mean?"

"I need some help," she said. "The other assistant, Ricky, was supposed to be here by now but who knows where that slacker is."

"What kind of help do you need?" Court asked.

"I need to lift the body onto the autopsy table," she said. "It's not difficult—just heavy."

Mel looked to Tom, who was conveniently reviewing his notes, but then Court surprised her by volunteering.

"I'll do it," she said. "Do I get gloves?"

"If you insist," Jordan said with a kidding smirk.

She nodded in the direction of the instrument table, where a box of latex gloves sat on the bottom shelf. Court went over and retrieved a pair, and Jordan told her to put on a paper gown, too.

"It ties up the back," she said. "Some people have to be told."

Court put her arms through the gown, and then Mel stepped behind her. "Here, let me."

"Thanks," she said, lifting her golden hair out of the way. Mel got a waft of coconut, warm and sweet, and as she fumbled with the ties, her fingers were suddenly a little clumsy. It felt like the process was taking longer than it should have—there were only three ties—and when she finally finished, she noticed that Tom and Jordan were both staring at the two of them.

"All set?" Jordan asked, a playful grin on her lips.

Oh great, Mel thought. She hadn't had a ton of experience at the medical examiner's office, but she did know from Zara that Jordan had a reputation as a prankster, and you did *not* want to be in her sights.

"Yes," Court said, turning to look at Mel. "Thanks."

"No problem," she said, then cleared her throat and stepped back.

Court went over to the autopsy table and Jordan told

CARA MALONE

her where to stand and what to do. She unzipped the
body bag, and together they lifted the deceased onto the
table. It was a thin-looking woman who appeared to be in
her late fifties or early sixties. Even from where she stood
a dozen feet away, Mel could see the abundance of track
marks on her arm.

She wondered if Zara had ever crossed paths with
this woman. Fox County, like much of the rest of the
country, was in the middle of an opiate epidemic, and in
the narcotics department, Zara was doing everything in
her power to stop it. Still, some people slipped through
the proverbial cracks.

"Shame," Tom said, shaking his head, and Mel
jumped slightly—she'd completely forgotten he was
there, standing beside her.

"Yeah," she agreed.

Jordan had just finished prepping the body when the
second autopsy assistant, Ricky, appeared.

"So good of you to show up," Jordan said. "*After* I did
all your work for you."

"I brought you a smoothie, it's in the break room
fridge," Ricky said by way of apology, and Jordan gave a
grudging thanks.

Then Drs. Trace and Hanson arrived, along with the
forensic investigators assigned to the two cases, and
everyone gowned and gloved up. Dr. Hanson began his
examination of the deceased woman at the back autopsy
table, and Dr. Trace led her team out to the garage.

"Police cadet?" she asked when she noticed that
Court wasn't in a uniform beneath her paper gown.

"Hopeful," she said. "I'm just shadowing Tom, err, Detective Logan on this case."

"She's a dispatcher," he said. "Hoping to move up the ladder."

Mel introduced herself as well, explaining that she'd responded to the scene last night and realizing that she had no good excuse for being here now. She wasn't hoping to make detective, nor did she have any vested interest in the case. Luckily, Dr. Trace was more concerned with the fact that she had a heavy workload today and she didn't ask about her.

The five of them—Mel, Court, Tom and Jordan, along with a day shift investigator named Tyler—followed Dr. Trace while she walked around the entire burned vehicle, making observations. Tyler took notes on a tablet.

"Decedent appears to have been in the passenger seat," Dr. Trace said, "and is slumped with head in the direction of the driver's seat. Extensive full-thickness burns are evident on the skin, with a burn pattern consistent with use of a fire accelerant."

It took about twenty minutes for her to finish making observations of the body inside the vehicle. Then Jordan and Tyler extracted it and took it into the morgue on a gurney, the rest of the group followed them back inside. Dr. Trace and Jordan performed pre-autopsy X-rays and the doctor's face lit up when they found hardware on the decedent's knee joint.

"You said you got the name of the vehicle owner, right, Detective Logan?" she asked.

He nodded. "Eric Gilles."

"We can request medical records for Gilles," she said. "If he had a knee replacement, we'll be able to compare the X-rays to make a positive identification, or rule him out if not. I'll put in the request right now, and we should have an answer back soon."

She went over to a computer at a desk near the door, and while she submitted the request, Jordan and Tyler moved the body to the first autopsy table in the row. Mel noticed that Dr. Hanson was much farther along in his own examination, and that the woman with the track marks now had an open abdominal cavity.

The sight momentarily turned her stomach. She wasn't the queasy type, especially not after everything she'd seen on the job, but for just a second, because of the age of the decedent, she'd imagined her nonna on a steel table, her abdomen flayed open.

She's dying of cancer, Mel reminded herself. *They don't autopsy cancer victims.*

"Hey," Court said softly, one gloved hand going to Mel's elbow to steady her. "You okay?"

Mel immediately straightened up, drawing a deep breath to clear her head. "Yeah, fine."

Court retracted her hand. Mel had been perhaps a bit more curt than she needed to be, but how was she supposed to explain it? *I'm sorry, I'm sensitive about being pitied and needing help because I'm about to lose the only blood relative I have left.* She couldn't say all of that to a woman she just met in person a few hours ago.

No, she'd just leave her slightly crisp tone unacknowledged and hope that Court hadn't noticed.

Dr. Trace met the rest of them at the autopsy table, saying that the medical records request had been submitted, and proceeded with the rest of the external examination. There was no evidence of injury or other physical defects, but the extensive burns could well have destroyed any that had been present.

They moved on somewhat swiftly to the internal examination, and this time Mel didn't miss a beat when Dr. Trace made the Y-shaped incision down the torso. Court, standing right beside her, leaned in a little closer to get a better look, and Mel was amused at that.

Who *was* this girl who made such quick work of breaking down her professional defenses, who was so easy to talk to, who made Mel want more... and who apparently didn't bat an eyelash at the prospect of moving corpses and getting right into the splash zone during an autopsy?

Mel didn't even know her last name, and yet she was intrigued.

The internal autopsy showed no evidence of smoke inhalation or burning to the lung tissue, which Dr. Trace said indicated that the decedent had died before the fire began. Otherwise, there was nothing of note, no abnormalities, injuries or signs of illness.

About an hour after the exam began, Dr. Trace was stitching the abdominal cavity back up when the ancient fax machine near the computer came to life and started

CARA MALONE

printing out sheets of paper. She said, "That'll be Eric Gilles' medical records, I bet."

"May I?" Tom asked, and she smiled.

"Are you telling me you know how to read a radiograph?"

"No, but I can read a patient file," he said. "I just wanna know if Gilles had a knee replacement. If the answer is no, then nobody needs to read the radiograph."

"I doubt they would have even bothered to fax the records if he hadn't," Dr. Trace pointed out. "But be my guest."

Tom went over to the fax machine, scanning the pages while Dr. Trace and Jordan finished closing the body. "Well?" she asked.

"Right knee was replaced in 2003," he read. "Gilles was a veteran, served in Iraq and was discharged after he blew out his knee during a training exercise in Baghdad. Bad luck."

"The timeframe sounds about right for what we saw on the X-rays," Dr. Trace said. "I'll make sure the serial numbers match to be sure, but it sounds like Gilles is your man."

"So, what's the cause of death?" Court asked, then immediately clamped her lips shut and looked guiltily at Tom.

Keep your eyes open and your mouths shut. That's what he'd said, and Mel couldn't help finding it cute how chastised Court looked before he'd even turned his head her way.

"Inconclusive," Dr. Trace said. "I can say with

reasonable certainty that the victim did not die in the fire, but given the extensive burning, I can't make a determination of cause or manner of death at this time. I'll send blood and tissue samples to the lab later today, and maybe the results will shed more light on the case."

"So, what happens now?" Court asked, pushing her luck again.

"Now, we pound the pavement," Tom said. "Talk to people who knew Eric Gilles, try to get a last known location and figure out what was going on in his life before he died."

CHAPTER SEVEN
COURT

*O*utside the medical examiner's office, Tom stopped on the sidewalk to make a call to the police station, so Court and Mel stood by the car and waited.

It was sunny, a little past noon, and Court had to stifle a yawn. Ordinarily she'd be in her bed in the finished half of her parents' basement, where she'd moved after she started working the night shift and quickly realized how hard it was to sleep during the day. At least down there, the cool cinderblock walls muffled the neighborhood sounds and it was easier to block the light from the small egress windows than from the big bay window in her old bedroom.

She'd be dead to the world by this time most other days, but even though her body was protesting, sleep was the last thing on her mind right now.

She was still thinking about everything she'd just seen, puzzling over the mystery of just how Eric Gilles had died if the fire hadn't killed him... and admiring the cute officer beside her who was still wearing her police blues.

"Have you observed autopsies before?" Court asked.

"One," Mel said. "In the police academy. They want everyone to see one because it helps desensitize you for when you inevitably encounter a body in the field." She smiled at Court and added, "Not that you'll have any problem with that. You're not squeamish at all, are you?"

"Blood and guts don't bother me," Court said. "Besides, I hear all kinds of crazy shit working dispatch—sometimes imagining it and not being able to see it seems even worse than being there."

"I don't know about that," Mel said with a smile that brought out her dimple again. Her long, straight ponytail hung over one shoulder, and the early afternoon breeze picked up a few stray tendrils and whipped them across her face. One hand went absently up to try to smooth them back down, but a few dark hairs clung to her lower lip.

"Here," Court said, taking a step closer and hooking one finger over the stray hairs. "Caught in your lip gloss, don't you hate that?"

"ChapStick," Mel corrected, then nodded. "But yeah."

Court's fingertips brushed the side of Mel's neck, soft and warm, and she could swear she felt her pulse for just a second. It was quick, and their eyes locked. Court smiled and her heart fluttered in her chest. Then she stepped back again.

"There. Got them."

"Thank you," Mel said. She ran her hands through her ponytail, cleaning off any ChapStick that may have been transferred in the process. Court damn near opened her mouth to say that Mel's pretty face matched the kindness that Court had picked up in her voice on the radio.

But then Tom walked over, saying, "I got the address for Gilles' next of kin—his mother. You two tagging along?"

Mel looked to Court, but Court didn't miss a beat. "I'm in for as long as you'll let me."

"Me too, then," Mel added.

"Good, that's one less trip I have to make by not dropping you two at the precinct," Tom said. He hit the unlock button on his key fob, then grumbled, "Although I don't know how I keep getting saddled with rookies and detective hopefuls."

"It's probably your sparkling personality," Court suggested. "People are just drawn to you."

Mel let out a snort as she got into the car. Court joined her in the back because Tom had all his notes and several days' worth of fast food trash taking up the front passenger seat.

"Does Gilles' mother know he's dead yet?" Court asked.

"No," Tom grunted. "That's one of the worst things about this job. Watching an autopsy is a walk in the park compared to having to notify the family and then stick around to try to get answers out of them. If you can handle that, then you're ready to take the civil service exam."

"Is that what this is?" Mel asked. "A trial run before you commit?"

"Oh, I know I want to be a cop," Court said, biting her tongue just before she accidentally confessed the reason why she hadn't taken the plunge yet. She was really starting to like Mel, and she didn't need her turning into one of two things that so many people became when they found out her dad was the chief: a suck-up or a ghost.

"Why haven't you signed up for the academy yet?" Mel asked when Court didn't volunteer any further information. "You've been working dispatch for a couple of years now, right?"

Court had to smile. Did Mel know that just from recognizing the sound of her voice? She must, because the dispatchers didn't go around announcing themselves to the patrol officers—they were too busy coordinating response teams.

"Yeah," Court said. "I guess the timing just hasn't been right yet."

Now, that one wasn't *really* a lie. She'd just omitted the fact that it was her father's timing that was holding her up, not her own. Court found Tom's eyes in the rearview mirror, telepathically begging him not to let the whole *chief's daughter* thing slip.

"Well, you should go for it," Mel said. "I mentioned my previous partner, Zara Hayes, earlier—she wanted to be a narcotics detective so badly, but it took her a while to move up because the chief didn't think she was ready. The minute she convinced him, though, she went for it and she's never been happier."

Court smirked inwardly. So she wasn't the only one her dad fussed over... she wasn't sure if that made her feel better or not.

"If you're the only one holding yourself back, you should go for it too," Mel said.

She was looking at Court with a smile that said she believed in her, a funny feeling since they'd only met in person a few hours ago, and yet Court was sure she was sincere.

"Thanks," she said. "Maybe I will."

---

*E*ric Gilles' mother lived in a tiny house on the rough side of town, in a neighborhood that had once been thriving, back when downtown Fox City was booming with factory jobs. Now everything was automated or outsourced, and the once blue-collar community here was struggling.

The house that Tom parked in front of had dented, baby blue aluminum siding and moss was growing on the roof, but the yard was well-kept with flowers growing in beds in front of the small porch.

Tom killed the engine on his car, then turned around to face Mel and Court.

"You two just be polite and quiet in there, okay?" he said. "If she asks, Mel, you're an officer assigned to the case..." He glanced at Court, wearing the black slacks and polo shirt that served as her dispatch uniform. "...and you're a cadet in training, Court. She doesn't need to know you're not actually in the academy yet."

"Okay," Court agreed, a little quiver of nerves announcing itself in her stomach. "So, what do we do in there?"

"Nothing," Tom said. "I'll do all the talking." He rummaged in the pile of papers on the front passenger seat, then handed her a small flip-style notebook. "You can take notes if you want."

Court's eyes lit up and she smiled at Mel, who looked amused. It was just a notebook—a battered one at that—but it was the first active thing she was being permitted to do during an investigation... if she didn't count helping Jordan move that body in the morgue.

Mel just smiled back, and Tom handed Court a pen. Then they all got out of the car and walked up the short sidewalk to the little blue house.

Eric's mother—Lydia Gilles, as Tom had identified her—was a somewhat haggard-looking woman in her late sixties, who came to the door in a pair of sweatpants and a loose T-shirt.

"Yes?" she said, pushing her graying hair away from her forehead. Tom showed her his badge and identified himself, as well as Mel and Court, and before he even had the chance to tell her why they were there, her face broke into an expression of agony and she asked, "Is this about Rachel?"

"Rachel?" Tom asked, surprised.

"My daughter," the woman said. "She's in the hospital. I just got home an hour ago—did something happen?"

Court's stomach dropped and she glanced at Mel. They were standing side by side behind Tom, and if it weren't totally unprofessional, Court would have reached over to squeeze Mel's hand. She looked like her heart was breaking for Lydia Gilles and the news she was about to receive.

"No, ma'am," Tom said. "I'm sorry, but I'm here about your son, Eric."

"Oh God," the woman said. "Is he..."

She couldn't finish asking the question.

"He's dead," Tom confirmed, his tone gentler than Court had known he was capable of. He also looked ready to catch Lydia if she ended up fainting. She clutched the doorframe, but somehow remained standing.

After a moment, the woman composed herself and stood upright again. Court could tell she was struggling to rein in the emotion in her voice as she asked, "I suppose you want to come in?"

"We don't want to impose," Tom said. "I do have just a few questions for you, though. I can ask them here on the porch if you prefer."

Lydia thought for a beat, then sighed. "No, you better come in because I really need to sit down. Come on."

She turned and walked away from the door, leaving Tom, Court and Mel to follow her. Inside, the house was dark, without a lot of natural light coming in. There was a small hallway with stairs to the right and a doorframe a few feet down on the left, where Lydia was leading them.

As she walked, she seemed to be running on autopilot, asking, "Can I get you anything? Water, soda?"

"No, ma'am, thank you," Tom answered for all three of them.

They went through the doorway, which led to a living room full of old but well-kept furniture arranged around a TV. Lydia dropped down in a recliner, then waved limply in the direction of the sofa. Court, Mel and Tom all sat, and Court flipped to a blank page in the notebook, trying to be discreet about it.

"We're very sorry for your loss, Mrs. Gilles," Tom said. "And I'm sorry to hear about your daughter. Would you mind my asking why she's in the hospital?"

"She had a fall," Lydia said. "Yesterday afternoon. Tripped and hit her head on the corner of the kitchen island."

"What's her prognosis?" Tom asked.

"She's unconscious right now," Lydia said. "I was with her all night, but I finally came home to take a shower." She looked down at her sweatpants. "Obviously, I didn't get that far."

"I'm sorry," Tom said. "I know the news about Eric must come as a shock to you on top of your daughter's injury."

"Not particularly," she said, her voice cracking as she lifted the hem of her oversized T-shirt to use as a tissue for the tears pooling in her eyes. Tom waited patiently for her to continue, and she looked up after a moment, explaining, "Eric's been struggling for a while now. Was it an overdose?"

Mel cut a surprised look toward Court, but Tom kept his expression neutral and asked, "Your son was addicted to drugs?"

Lydia nodded. "Heroin. He'd get clean for a while, start to turn things around, but then something would always set him off and he'd go back to the drugs." Her voice cracked again and this time she couldn't stop herself from openly crying as she said, "I've been praying for twenty years that he would overcome that demon, but a little part of me always knew this was how it would end."

Tom turned to Mel and mouthed *tissues,* and she found the box he was motioning toward on the end table to her left. She picked it up and offered it to Lydia, who cradled it in her lap like a baby while the tears continued to fall.

"When was his most recent relapse?" Tom asked gently.

Lydia plucked a tissue from the box, struggling to compose herself. She dabbed at her cheeks, blew her nose, and took a deep breath. Then she looked Tom in the eyes again, regaining the determined calm that she'd first drawn upon in the doorway.

"I haven't seen him in about a week," she said. "He usually comes around once or twice a week to have dinner, and if he doesn't show up, that's my sign that he's probably struggling again. I called him last night after Rachel's accident but he didn't pick up the phone. I was going to go over to his apartment to check on him after my shower. Oh God, he wasn't..." She winced, no doubt imagining awful things. "How long was he dead before someone found him?"

Court looked at Tom. She didn't envy him right now, having to share this news with a grieving mother, especially one who already had one child in crisis.

He told Lydia about the vehicle fire, being honest while glossing over the gorier details, and he told her that they believed Eric was already dead before the fire was set. Hopefully that would provide some small amount of comfort. But as Tom related all that information, Lydia's face slowly contorted into horror.

"So you're saying my son was murdered?"

"We're not able to make that determination at this time," Tom said. "It could have been an overdose, and whoever was with him panicked and tried to conceal what happened. Do you have any ideas who that could be... his dealer, maybe?"

Lydia shook her head. "I don't know anybody from that part of Eric's life. Vee might."

"Vee?"

"His wife," she said, and this time, Tom couldn't hide his surprise.

His eyebrows rose as he asked, "Eric was married?"

"Divorced," she said, then shrugged. "Or, well, estranged I guess. I don't know if they ever got the legal aspect handled, what with Eric's addiction. He tried so hard, but he just could never get his life together, not after that damn war."

"Was that when the addiction began?" Tom asked. "When he came back from Iraq?"

"Yes," she said. "He had surgery and they gave him morphine while he was recovering. This was before people really understood how easy it could be to become dependent, and he was in so much pain. He also..."

She trailed off, dabbed at her eyes with a fresh tissue, and Tom gently prompted her. "I'm sorry, I realize you have a lot to deal with right now and we won't keep you much longer, but you were going to say something?"

She shook her head. "It's nothing. I was just going to say that the morphine wasn't the only thing that changed him—he seemed different even before the surgery. But who can go to war and come back unscathed? You'd have to be a sociopath or something not to be affected by that."

"He saw combat, then?" Tom asked gently.

Mrs. Gilles nodded. "Some, although his platoon was mostly there to prevent the looting that went on in Baghdad after Hussein was captured."

"Well, I'm so sorry for your loss, Mrs. Gilles," Tom said, standing and motioning for Mel and Court to do the same. "If you happen to have the contact information for Eric's wife, I'd really appreciate it, and then we'll get out of your hair."

She nodded and stood up, looking more like a zombie than a functioning human. She went back into the hallway and the three of them followed her to her purse hanging on the banister. She took out her phone and scrolled for a minute, then held it up to Tom.

"There's her phone number," she said. "Or, at least

the last one I've got for her. Can't guarantee she hasn't changed it—I never talk to her anymore."

"That's fine, thank you," Tom said, then asked Court to jot the number down. When she was finished, he said, "Thanks for your time, Mrs. Gilles. I hope Rachel recovers well."

"Me too," Lydia said. And they left her there in the dark hallway, clutching the railing at the bottom of the stairs and looking like she was about to collapse any minute.

Once they were outside, Court let out a shaky breath. "Jesus, that was awful."

"Still want to be a cop?" Tom asked grimly.

She took another breath, looked at Mel in her uniform, her badge reflecting the early afternoon sun, and found that yes, she did want that.

More than anything.

CHAPTER EIGHT

*L*ydia felt crunchy and exhausted, her T-shirt stained with tears and a small army of crumpled tissues scattered around her feet. She still hadn't gotten that shower, not to mention the nap she so sorely needed, but after the cops left her house, there was very little chance of that happening.

She went into the kitchen and started a pot of coffee —that would have to suffice because her to-do list just got a hell of a lot longer. Now she had funeral arrangements to think of, people to notify, an obituary to write...

For her son.

Even with all of his problems with addiction, Lydia had never actually allowed herself to imagine this day—a mother burying her son just wasn't supposed to happen. And she had a daughter lying unconscious in the ICU on top of that. Could life find any other ways to kick her in the kidneys right now?

Well... there was one thing that could put Lydia in a worse mood than she was in right now.

Vee Gilles. Or Mayfair, if she was going by her maiden name again.

Just thinking about her made Lydia clench her jaw, and yet she figured that as much as she hated her, she owed the damn woman a courtesy call after she'd given her name to the cops.

"Sonofabitch," she grumbled as she took the coffee pot out of the percolator before it even finished brewing, pouring herself a cup of extra-strong coffee as droplets sizzled on the hot plate. She shoved the pot back in its place and took a sip, then went over to the table in one corner of the kitchen and sat down.

She set her phone down next to her cup, scrolling through the contacts, looking for Vee for the second time in an hour. When was the last time she'd spoken to the woman? Years, definitely.

And then, a memory came, unbidden. The last time Lydia could remember seeing Vee was the night she'd practically dumped Eric on her doorstep, high as a kite and sobbing because he wanted to make the marriage work and Vee didn't. They'd been separated by that point, and Vee had moved about an hour away for work. When she rang Lydia's doorbell that night, she'd said that Eric took a bus out to see her, to beg her to take him back, and the minute she saw his dilated pupils she'd stuffed him in the car and driven him back to Fox City.

Lydia couldn't exactly blame her for that part. They'd all been begging Eric to get help for years at that point, and he could only ever seem to stay sober for little chunks of time. Something always knocked him off the wagon.

But Lydia had seen the cold, unfeeling look in Vee's eyes as she told Eric, right there on Lydia's stoop, that she was done with his problems and the next time, he could find his own way home. And Lydia *could* blame her for that. Whatever happened to 'for better or worse'?

Well, she thought as the phone rang, *the 'til death do you part' element is still correct.*

"Hello?" The voice on the other end of the line sounded testy, right off the bat.

"Veronica?" Lydia's voice came out weak, frail like her grandmother's had been toward the end. She hated that she couldn't muster anything stronger.

"Yeah," Vee said, impatient. "What's going on, Lydia?"

"I don't know how to say this..." *Just say it,* she told herself. *The sooner you say it, the sooner this call ends.* "Eric's gone."

The line went silent for a long moment, and Lydia was surprised to find herself wishing that they were having this conversation in person. As much as she begrudged Eric's wife leaving him when he most needed her, Lydia wished she could see Vee's reaction right now. Was she sad? Sorry? Relieved?

Was it horrible that somewhere, deep down inside herself, Lydia was a tiny bit relieved? The demons that had been hounding her son for so many years would finally let him rest. That was something, as insignificant as it felt in the moment.

At last, Vee said, "Lydia, I'm so sorry."

Again, Lydia couldn't quite read her emotions. "I just found out," she went on, determined to say what she had to and get on with things. "I know you don't have anything to do with him anymore, and that's your right..."

God, she hated to say that. She could still vividly remember the night Vee walked out on Eric. Lydia had come over to their house to deliver dinner, a tuna casserole, and found Eric strung out and Vee packing her things. They fought, the casserole dish got dropped and broken, and Lydia got angry. Vee was Eric's wife—you don't just leave someone you love when things get tough.

Lydia could still remember what Vee had shouted at her on her way out the door. *I deserve a husband who's not going to OD in the middle of the night and count on me to sleep with one eye open to save him!* Then she'd slammed the door, and she was out of his life just like that.

Just like she'd never loved him at all.

And now he was dead.

"...I just wanted you to know because the police asked me for your contact information," Lydia continued, jaw tight. "And because you're still his wife, right?"

Vee's voice came back stonier than before. "Legally, yes. It was an overdose, I assume?"

That cold, unfeeling bitch.

"They burned him," Lydia blurted, allowing herself to think about it for the first time since the police told her.

"What?"

"They burned my boy."

"Who?"

"I don't know, Vee, you tell me!" Suddenly, she was spitting mad. She was just trying to do the decent thing, give Vee a heads-up, and here she was, pumping Lydia for information as if she were rubbernecking at the scene of a traffic accident. If she wanted to know these things, she should have stuck around!

"Excuse me?" Vee has the nerve to snap back.

Oh, that was it... the gloves were coming off.

"You're the one who knew all his druggie friends, not me," Lydia growled. "If you wanted to know what was going on in my son's life, you would have asked *him,* and not waited until it was too late."

"Lydia–"

"Oh, that's right, I remember now," Lydia kept going, "You left him, but you couldn't be bothered to actually divorce him in all this time. You want to know what I think?" Lydia was sure Vee didn't, but she was going to hear it anyway. "I think you've been waiting for this day like a vulture, waiting to get your hands on his military pension!"

That money would have gone to Lydia if they'd gotten divorced. She did fine for herself, she didn't need the money... but the fact that Vee was legally entitled to it made Lydia feel sick to her stomach.

And now, given the silence on the other end of the line, it seemed like Vee wasn't even going to make an effort to defend herself. Despicable.

At last, Vee answered, her voice flat and emotionless once again. "I'm very sorry for your loss, Lydia, but I'm on my lunch break and have to get back to work. Thank you for letting me know."

"You're welcome," Lydia answered, in a tone that meant anything but that.

Then the line went dead, and she found herself seething, nearly crying, staring at a cup of coffee that would turn her stomach now if she tried to drink it. She had a lot more calls to make and things to do, but for now, she just really needed a damn shower.

Lydia got up from the table, dumped her undrunk coffee in the sink, and walked down the hall to the shower, barely mustering the energy to lift her feet as she went.

CHAPTER NINE
MEL

*I*t was the early afternoon when Tom pulled back into the police station parking garage. He pretty swiftly dispensed with his two shadows by explaining the boring paperwork and phone calls that came next in the investigation.

Mel was starting to get pretty tired by then anyway, despite all the excitement—it was nearly eight hours past her usual bedtime, and she could tell from the way Court kept turning her head to stifle yawns that she was in pretty much the same condition.

"What do you say we part ways for now?" Tom suggested. "I'll let you both know the next time I'm about to do something interesting."

"Promise you won't go without us?" Court asked, and Mel smiled.

She'd only gone to Tom's desk this morning because she wanted to impress her dispatcher friend, and when she'd found out that Court was that dispatcher, there was no real reason for her to keep following the case. She'd been tagging along all day simply because she was looking for a distraction and Court was one hell of a pretty and intriguing one. It felt nice to hear her say 'us,' to know Court was thinking of her too.

"I know you'd have my head on a stick if I did," Tom said as the three of them walked over to the elevators. Tom was headed to his desk, and Mel and Court both had to punch out at the time clock before they could go home.

The whole way up, Court was pumping Tom for information—who was he going to call? What was his theory on the case? What did he make of the fact that the victim's sister had been admitted to the hospital on the same night he died?

It was all interesting—probably more interesting than the things Mel saw on an average night on patrol—but what she was really focused on in that moment was how tightly packed they were in that tiny, ancient elevator. How Court's shirtsleeves brushed Mel's when she gestured, and the coconut scent of her hair wafted over as she talked.

Warm. Sweet. Inviting.

Mel was always secretly excited to talk to Court over the radio, but in person she was even better. After their first day together, Mel knew she was nursing a crush.

When the elevator stopped and the doors slid open, Tom waved goodbye and made a beeline for his desk, probably thrilled to be rid of the two of them for a while so he could focus on his work. Mel followed Court to the time clock mounted on the wall near the break room, where Court punched out then waited for Mel.

While she was entering her badge number, the chief came out of the break room with a donut in one hand, a cup of coffee in the other. Court made a quick, funny step, as if she was trying to hide behind Mel, and Mel wondered if she was worried they would get in trouble for being here so long after their shifts had ended.

It wasn't like they would actually get overtime for following Tom around—they just had to be clocked in so the station knew where they were in case anything happened to them.

Mel opened her mouth, about to explain that to her, when the chief said, "Courtney, what are you still doing here?"

And the weirdest part about the whole thing was that he tucked the donut behind his back—he was hiding it from her!

She stepped out from behind Mel and held her hand out, demanding, "Donut. Now."

The chief let out a sigh and handed it to her, and suddenly everything clicked into place for Mel. Everybody knew the chief had a daughter who worked at the station, and that his wife had been a cop too, once upon a time. Mel just never knew the details until now.

"Oh my God," she murmured, thinking about all the inappropriate things she'd done in the last twelve hours with the chief's daughter—things that could get her fired. *Shit!*

She finished punching out and turned on her heels,

her cheeks burning with embarrassment as she marched back to the elevators. Behind her, she heard Court saying, "Have a good day, Dad, I have to go." And before Mel could slip inside the elevator and punch the 'Door Close' button, Court was waving her hand over the sensor, keeping it open.

"Hey," she said, looking sheepish. "Can I ride back down with you?"

"Yeah," Mel said, stepping to the side. "Of course."

How rude and awkward would it have been to say no?

Court got in and pushed the button to take them back to the parking garage. The doors slid shut, and she turned to Mel. "So, uh, my dad's the chief."

"Yeah, I gathered that," Mel said.

"Are you mad?"

"More like mortified," Mel confessed. "I never would have promised to keep you in the loop on that case if I knew you were the chief's daughter. Why didn't you tell me?"

Court just looked at her with those big, gorgeous eyes, sadness reflected in them.

"Oh. Right," Mel said, figuring it out for herself. "Because I never would have promised."

Court nodded. "I hate being treated differently by everybody who knows who my dad is. I'm just a dispatcher who wants to be a cop someday, and that's who I wanted you to see me as—myself, not the chief's daughter."

"I get that," Mel said. "I understand."

"Forgive me?" Court asked, and with those doe eyes and the slight pout of her lip, there was honestly not much in the world Mel wouldn't have forgiven her for.

"Yeah," Mel said. "I'm sorry I freaked a bit."

The elevator opened onto the parking garage and they stepped out. Court said, "For what it's worth, I would never go running to my dad about something a coworker did... especially a pretty lady like yourself."

She gave Mel a little smile, tentative but flirtatious, and it made the heat rise into her cheeks all over again. She hoped she wasn't outwardly blushing, but if she was, Court might just think that was the natural color of her face because she hadn't stopped feeling that way since they met.

"Wanna split this donut with me?" Court asked, gesturing to the chocolate cake donut still in her hand. "We missed lunch."

Mel's stomach growled at the mere mention of food. "We sure did." She nodded assent.

Court broke the donut in half and handed a piece to Mel. They wandered through the parking garage while they ate, and Mel wondered if they were heading toward Court's car. They sure as hell weren't walking toward her own, parked two levels down.

"My dad has the world's most ridiculous sweet tooth," Court explained. "And he's pretty much completely given up on trying to control it—stress of the job and all. I try to keep an eye on his diet when I can."

"That's thoughtful of you."

"He's all I've got left," she said.

There was a pang in Mel's chest, a physical ache. Court was so young to say something so sad, and yet Mel knew exactly what she meant. "My grandma's all I've got left," she said, "and she's not doing well lately."

It was the first time she'd talked about her grandmother to anyone other than her doctors and the in-home care nurses. It felt good to get that weight off her chest, and at the same time it made the chocolate donut turn to cardboard on her tongue.

But then, suddenly, Court's arms were enveloping her. She'd pulled Mel into such an abrupt hug that she'd dropped her own piece of donut on the ground. She squeezed her tight, an earnest hug, not one of those polite ones that you could barely feel. And Mel surprised herself by hugging Court back.

"I'm so sorry," Court said, her voice vibrating in Mel's ear. "I know how hard it is to lose someone you love."

Her mother. Of course.

Mel didn't know the details, just that she'd died in the line of duty.

"I'm sorry for your loss too," she said, the words coming out weak and ineffective. Were any words ever enough for a heartache like that?

They just held each other right there in the parking garage for another minute, and that felt so much better than any words of solace ever could. Then Court stepped back, smiled, looked bashful as she said, "Sorry. People tell me I wear my heart on my sleeve, and I can get kinda touchy-feely."

"Well, don't let it happen again," Mel said with a

stern look, "or I'll have to tell the chief I've been sexually harassed."

Court laughed. It lit up her whole face and echoed through the concrete parking structure. God, she was beautiful.

"Okay, and then I'll tell him you insinuated yourself in a case just to impress me," she said, then arched an eyebrow. "Am I right? Is that why you came along today?"

Mel's heart was pounding in her ears. She definitely had a crush, and it was turning out to be a big one. "Yes," she confessed. "Obviously it was totally unnecessary the minute I saw you at Tom's desk—you had your own source of information. But I wanted to spend time with you."

Her honesty was rewarded. Court leaned forward, her hand snaking around Mel's back and sending a shiver of curious anticipation through her. Then she plucked Mel's phone from her back pocket and held it out to her.

"Unlock," she demanded, and Mel put her finger to the biometric sensor. The phone unlocked and Court started typing, saying, "Here's my phone number, because I wouldn't mind spending a little more time with you—without all the homicide investigation stuff."

She handed the phone back with a smile that Mel struggled to return. She was in awe of this woman, who'd just taken charge in a way Mel never would have had the guts to do.

"Call me whenever you want," Court said. Then,

with one more sultry smile, she turned and walked over to her car, just a few parking spots away.

Mel turned and started walking back the other way, toward the elevator and the actual level her car was parked on. Her pulse was still racing and she hoped Court wouldn't see the dopey grin plastered across her face as she drove by.

CHAPTER TEN
COURT

*C*ourt walked away from Mel in that parking garage feeling pretty damn confident, and at home in her basement bedroom about an hour later, she was wide awake. Even with all the blackout curtains drawn, and in spite of the fact that she was eight hours overdue for sleep, she just couldn't bring herself to unwind.

Two things were running through her mind.

One, the Gilles case—she'd felt like a bona fide police officer today, even if she was only walking in Tom's footsteps.

And two, even more enticing, Mel. Court had liked her on the radio, but she was enthralled by her in person. What kept her awake was wondering if Mel felt the same way.

Luckily, she didn't have to wait long to find out. Court finally managed to sleep a few hours and went back to the station for her shift that night, yawned her way through it, but Mel wasn't on patrol so she didn't have the opportunity to figure out if the feeling was mutual. Then, at last, when her shift ended and she checked her phone, there was a text waiting for her.

Hey, it's Mel... haven't heard anything from Tom on the case yet, have you?

Court smiled. She knew Mel didn't care as much as she did about the Gilles case—this had to be just an excuse to reach out. She replied, *Nothing major, he's working with an arson investigator on the vehicle.* Then, after a moment's pause, she added, *What are you up to this morning?*

Since Mel hadn't worked last night, Court figured she would be well-rested and probably not heading straight to bed this morning. That was what Court should be doing herself, but she was always willing to sacrifice sleep for a pretty girl.

You might think it's silly, came the reply.

Court grinned, imagining all the silly things Mel could possibly be doing. Early morning ballroom dancing lessons? Feeding penguins at the zoo? Following another case and another cute dispatcher?

As long as it wasn't the last one, Court could live with it.

Tell me, she prompted.

There's a flea market that sets up every Saturday in the summer, out by the lake. I try go whenever I can.

Court answered, *That doesn't seem too silly.*

And she was pleasantly surprised when Mel answered back quickly, *Does that mean you want to come with?*

Yes, Court answered. Hell yes.

And that was how she found herself wandering through row after row of flea market vendors on the pier when she should have been sleeping.

She met Mel at the entrance about an hour after their texts, and smiled broadly when she saw Mel holding two extra tall coffee cups. She handed one to Court and said, "I figured you might need this—you worked last night, right?"

"Yep, and I most certainly appreciate it," she answered, taking the cup. When her fingers accidentally brushed Mel's, she didn't pull back right away. She let them linger for just a second longer, then thanked her and took a long, satisfied sip. "So, why the flea market? Do you have some kind of eBay antiques side hustle?"

"No, nothing like that," Mel said as she led Court into the fray. "Have you ever heard of Degenhart owls?"

Court furrowed her brow. "Can't say that I have."

"They're little glass figurines, about three inches tall," Mel explained. "Always poured from the same mold, but they come in all kinds of colors—made by an artist in Ohio from the 1940s to the 70s. Elizabeth Degenhart."

"And you're a collector?"

"My grandmother is," Mel said. "She's got almost a complete set."

Her smile faded, so subtly Court would have missed

it if she hadn't already been studying Mel's face instead of looking where she was walking.

"And you're trying to find the missing pieces for her–"

"Look out," Mel said, looping her arm in Court's and pulling her out of harm's way right before she collided with a stack of antique-looking wooden crates that had been piled at the end of a vendor table.

"Sorry!" Court said, waving to the vendor. "Whew, that could have been an expensive bout of clumsiness."

"Nah, those aren't real antiques," Mel said quietly into her ear as they kept walking. "You develop an eye for that kind of thing the more you come out here."

"Have you been looking for a while?"

Mel nodded, and the fact that she made no attempt to unlink their arms made Court's belly warm and tingly. As they walked, they scanned the tables—Mel knew what she was looking for, Court just tried to be helpful. And Mel explained, "Nonna's got all the widely available owls. There's this Carnival Cobalt one with a pretty metallic sheen that we've never been able to find, and a creamy yellow one called Custard Opal…"

She named off a few more colors, and Court asked, "Have you tried looking online?"

Mel gave her a scandalized look. "That's cheating."

Court laughed. "No, it's not!"

"Well, it is to Nonna and me," Mel explained. "We've been scouring flea markets off and on for years, ever since I was a kid. The hunt is half the fun, and I know she'd want to be out here with me now, but she's too sick. I figure completing the collection for her is the next best thing."

Court slid her hand down to twine her fingers in Mel's. "I'm sorry she's not doing well. What's she got?"

"Ovarian cancer," Mel said. Suddenly, her voice was flat, containing none of the emotion with which she'd just been talking about the owl hunt. Court recognized it—she'd switched over to the same mechanical tone whenever she had to talk about her mother for years after she passed.

"I'm sorry," she repeated, wishing she had something better to say.

"She's seventy-two and the chemo is kicking her ass," Mel went on. "She's a tough woman but her doctors say it's only a matter of time."

"I'm sure she's fighting like hell," Court said. "If she's anything like you, she won't go down without a fight."

Mel smiled. "What do you know about me? We just met."

"True, but I know a lot about you," Court answered. "I'm good at reading between the lines. Ooh, is that a Degen-thingy?"

She pointed to a little blue glass owl on one of the tables and Mel chuckled, going over to pick it up. "Yep, this is a Degenhart." She turned it upside down so Court could see the maker's mark, a circled D molded into the base. "The glass molds were sold after Elizabeth died and more owls were produced, but the original mark was removed. Anything with a mark like this was made by Elizabeth herself, and that's all Nonna and I collect."

"So we found one," Court beamed. "Is it one you've been looking for?"

Mel smiled. "Nah, this is Milk Blue, it's pretty common."

Then she took ten dollars out of her pocket and went over to the vendor to buy it. When she came back, Court asked, "What did you do that for? I thought you said you have this one already."

Mel put the little glass owl in her hand. "It's for you— your first Degenhart owl. Welcome to the hunt."

Court turned it over in her palm, inspecting it like it was precious crystal, then she smiled broadly at Mel. "I love it, thank you."

Those pretty brown eyes were sparkling back at her, just as excited as Court was. She would have kissed her right then and there if Mel hadn't been right about the fact that they'd only *really* known each other for about a day. And the fact that there were about two hundred thrifters and antiquers milling about, passing them on both sides and shooting them mildly grumpy looks for holding up the foot traffic.

Court tucked the owl safely in her pocket, then took Mel's hand again. They walked around the pier for another hour and found a couple more owls, but none of them were the ones Mel and her grandmother needed. She didn't seem disappointed, though. As they made their way slowly back toward the parking lot, she said, "That's just how it goes. You come out and look because you never know when somebody's going to be here with

77

just the thing you're searching for... but you don't expect too much in the meantime."

Court pulled the Milk Blue owl from her pocket. "Well, I had a successful day in any case."

Mel smiled, not letting go of her hand even though they'd arrived at Court's car. "Me too."

"I'm going to put this on my dashboard," Court announced, unlocking her door and leaning inside to position the owl below her rear-view mirror. "I'll have to get some sticky tack or something to anchor it. You don't think that'll hurt anything, will it?"

Mel chuckled. "Your dashboard, maybe. Not the owl."

Court shrugged. "This car has been to hell and back, so I doubt a little sticky tack will be the thing that does it in." She stood upright again, hesitating for a moment before she added, "This was my mom's car. It's twenty years old now and has had damn near everything under the hood replaced, but I can't bring myself to trade it in." She laughed. "Hell, when it finally quits for good, I just might turn it into a lawn ornament or something."

Mel smiled. "That could be a fun project, turn it into a great big planter, or a habitat for wildlife."

Court nodded. "I bet my mom would have loved that."

She wondered how much Mel knew about her—probably not much if she hadn't even realized that Court was the chief's kid. She wanted to tell her about her mother, not just about the shoot-out that had taken her life but how she loved to bake, and that she'd taught Court how to twirl a baton when she was young, and that her favorite TV show had been *Night Court,* even though she spent every day doing similar work.

Mel had shared so much about her grandmother, and after their owl hunt, Court felt like she knew her. She should return the favor.

But as open and easy-going as Court was about everything else, her mother was the one raw nerve that never seemed to get any less sensitive.

"Well, thank you for inviting me to come along this morning," she said. "I had a lot of fun."

"Me too," Mel said. "The flea market is always better with company."

"I should get some sleep," Court said reluctantly. Being a responsible adult was for the birds. "I've got work tonight."

"I do too," Mel said. "I'll talk to you then." And, unexpectedly, she leaned in and planted a soft, sweet kiss on Court's lips. It was warm and wonderful, and entirely too short. Mel drew back slightly, her voice low and seductive as she said, "Sweet dreams."

Damn. How the hell was Court supposed to sleep now?

CHAPTER ELEVEN
MEL

*M*el had butterflies in her stomach by the time she sat down behind the wheel of her squad car that night and called in to let the dispatchers know she was available for assignment.

It wasn't a good headspace to be in. She was still floating from her time with Court that morning, and now —when her mind should be on her work—she was still thinking about her. Those big doe eyes. The curves of her body that Mel couldn't seem to stop stealing glimpses at. The coconut scent she caught whenever Court turned her head.

Damn it. It was a dangerous way for a solo patrol officer to feel.

Still, when Court's chipper voice came over the radio, answering, "Ten-four, Car 34," a sappy grin spread across Mel's face. Then she wiped it away and pulled out of the parking garage, determined to shut off that part of her brain for the night.

It was a pretty average shift. A handful of traffic stops, including one DUI. A homeless man loitering in a nice neighborhood where people didn't like to see that sort of thing. A teenage shoplifter caught trying to steal booze from an all-night convenience store. None of it was compelling enough to keep Mel's mind from fixating on her usual worry—Nonna—or her new fascination, Court.

So, around daybreak when her cell started to vibrate on the passenger seat, Mel was excited to see that Tom was calling. She snatched up the phone.

"Hey, what's going on?"

"I found out which hospital Eric Gilles' sister is being treated at," he said. "Gonna head over there this morning and see what I can find out. You want to tag along again?"

Is Court going to be there? That was Mel's first thought, but she was sure that Court wouldn't miss it. "Definitely," she said. "Meet at your desk again?"

"Sure," he said. "We'll head out about eight."

As soon as they'd hung up, Mel pulled to the side of the street and texted Court.

Tom just called about Gilles' sister. U going?

Court didn't text back right away—likely dispatching a call, although Mel didn't hear her on the radio. She pulled back onto the road, which was just beginning to get crowded as people began their morning commutes. And a few minutes later, her phone chimed.

Without pulling over this time, she glanced at the notification.

81

Wouldn't miss it—see you soon!

Mel smiled, then worked on turning the Court part of her brain off again for the last hour of her shift.

$\mathcal{T}$wo hours later, she was stepping out of an elevator at Fox County Hospital in the heart of downtown, Court at her side and Tom leading the way.

They were entering the intensive care unit, where dozens of monitors beeped from all around. The hallways were stark white and fluorescent while some of the patient rooms were dimmed or dark. The antiseptic smell that pervaded every floor of the hospital gave Mel flash-backs to taking Nonna to see her oncologist and, worse, sitting with her in that grim chemotherapy room full of medical-grade recliners as Nonna and half a dozen other patients got toxic chemicals pumped into their veins.

She gritted her teeth unconsciously, forcing her jaw to relax every time she noticed she was doing it again.

They went to the nurses' station, where Tom flashed his badge and said, "I called earlier about Rachel Tucker. I'm Tom Logan with Fox County PD."

"Yes, one of the other nurses spoke to you, but she told me to expect you," the woman behind the counter said. "Rachel's husband is with her now—I'll let him know you're here."

She got up and padded softly down the hall. The

ICU was a quiet place, like a library or a mausoleum…
until there was an emergency. Then all hell would break
loose. *Stop clenching your jaw,* Mel commanded herself,
and stole a glance at Court.

Her eyes had gone dark, the sparkle stolen right out
of them. Had her mother been in a place like this before
she died?

"Mr. Logan?"

Mel turned her attention back to the task at hand as a
man with a high and tight haircut and a weightlifter's
body came up the hall toward them, the nurse trailing
behind him. She ducked back behind the nurses' station,
and he held out his hand.

"I'm Adam Tucker, Rachel's husband."

"Detective Logan," Tom said. "These are my
associates, Officer Mel Pine and Courtney Wilson. I'm
sorry to hear about your wife. Is there somewhere we can
talk for a few minutes?"

Adam let out a weary sigh and glanced at the nurse,
then asked, "Okay if I bring them to Rachel's room?"

She nodded, and Adam turned abruptly and led the
way. Mel tried not to peek into the other rooms that they
passed, out of respect as well as a desire to avoid seeing
horrible things. But it was almost impossible to ignore the
siren call of all those beeping monitors.

They passed people on ventilators, people with rela-
tives keeping vigil, people who were clearly 'circling the
drain' in medical parlance. And in the room Adam led
them to, a woman lay unconscious in bed, her head
wrapped up in a bandage with brown, stringy hair

sticking out the top. Tubes and electrical leads were coming off her in all directions, connecting to her own litany of medical monitors.

"Rachel, there are some police officers here to talk to us," Adam said, then looked sheepishly at Tom and explained, "She's still unconscious but the doctor said we should talk to her as if she can hear us."

"Her mother said that she fell two days ago," Tom said. "Can you tell us what happened?"

"Freak accident," Adam said, taking a seat in a chair that had been pulled up to Rachel's bedside. There was only one more chair in the room, so Tom took it and Mel and Court stood near the door. "I found her lying on the floor in the kitchen when I came home from work, unconscious, blood gushing from her head."

Mel looked at Rachel, at the bandage around her head. She knew from what Tom had uncovered that Rachel was in her early thirties, but lying there like that, weak and inert, she could have been decades older. She wore a shapeless hospital gown and her hair was oily and unwashed. A pretty sapphire necklace peeking out from under her gown was the only evidence that she'd once been alert, vibrant, and apparently stylish.

"...cracked her skull on the corner of the kitchen island," Adam was saying. "Best I could figure, she'd been getting ready to take our dog for his evening walk and got tangled up in his leash. He's a puppy, just brought him home a few weeks ago, and he's got way too much energy. When I got home and found Rachel lying there, he was sitting by her side with his chin on his paws, like he knew what he did and he felt bad about the accident."

"Large breed?" Tom asked.

Adam nodded. "Samoyed." He narrowed his eyes at Tom, then asked, "Are you here because of Rachel, or because of Eric?"

"What do you know about what happened to Eric?" Tom asked.

"Just what Lydia told me," Adam said, rubbing his eyes. "You can ask the nurses, I've pretty much been living at the hospital ever since Rachel got admitted. I know Eric died."

"You don't sound particularly surprised about that," Tom observed.

"He had problems," Adam said. "Been on opiates and street drugs off and on ever since his knee surgery. I love the guy, but honestly, a little part of me has been bracing for this. I just never expected to get kicked in the balls twice in one day," he added, gesturing to his wife.

"You were close with your brother-in-law?" Tom asked.

Adam nodded. "We were in the service together. When we came back from Iraq, I didn't have a place to stay and Eric let me crash with him. That's how I met Rachel. If it wasn't for Eric, I never would have met the love of my life."

He picked up Rachel's limp hand, careful not to disturb the IV or any of the leads. Mel glanced at Court, wondering if she was the only one who thought Adam was laying it on a little thick at the end there. He'd been through hell and Mel knew better to stereotype people, but for a beefy ex-military guy, he sure was getting weepy.

Plus, what were the odds of losing your brother-in-law in such a violent way on the same day your wife trips over the dog's leash hard enough to put her in a coma?

Court was alert, soaking everything in, but her expression gave nothing away. She really would make a good cop one day.

"I'm sorry for your loss," Tom said, then casually added, "So you were here at the hospital all night after you found your wife unconscious?"

Adam narrowed his eyes immediately. "Yeah, I think I said that. Am I a suspect or something?"

"Asking these questions is just part of my job," Tom said. "I'm sure you want to find whoever burned your brother-in-law's body, right?"

"Dude," Adam said, his eyes cutting to his wife. "She might be able to hear you. Don't give her any more reasons not to wake up."

"I'm sorry."

Adam pressed his lips together, annoyed, then said, "Yes. I was here all night. Lydia can confirm that, as can all of Rachel's doctors and nurses."

"And would you mind if I speak to one of her doctors?" Tom asked, trying to be as gentle as possible. "You know, just checking all the boxes, it's a matter of procedure."

"Fine," Adam said. "But can you leave me and my wife alone now? I'm tired and I got a lot going on."

"Of course," Tom said, rising from the chair and extending his hand again. "Thank you for taking the time to speak with us."

He gestured Mel and Court out into the hallway and they went back to the nurses' station, where a different nurse was typing notes into a computer. Tom asked the nurse to page Rachel's primary doctor, then he turned to Mel and Court.

"Well, thoughts?"

"Suspicious timing," Court said, confirming Mel's own thoughts.

"He seemed sincere, though," she added.

Tom nodded. "I'll find out where he works, make sure he's been where he says he was for the last few days."

The doctor arrived a few minutes later, a woman who managed to look well-put-together and yet still had a frazzled air about her. She introduced herself as Dr. Lawrence, the neurologist overseeing Rachel Tucker's care.

"We won't keep you long," Tom said. "Just have a couple questions."

He asked about Rachel's prognosis—good as long as she regained consciousness in the next couple of days—and whether her injuries were consistent with the type of accident that Adam had described.

"I'm no forensic pathologist, but I've seen patients who were worse off than Rachel after simple trip-and-falls," Dr. Lawrence said.

Tom had a few more questions, mainly having to do with Adam's whereabouts on the night Eric died, and everything checked out. He thanked Dr. Lawrence, then walked with Mel and Court back to the bank of elevators.

While they rode down to the parking garage, alone and able to speak openly, he gave them his most candid thoughts on the case so far. "Okay, here's what I'm thinking," he started, flipping through his notes. "It's highly unlikely that Eric died and his sister had a serious head injury in the same twenty-four-hour period *and* the two incidents weren't related in some way. Could be, but I've been around long enough to know how slim the odds are."

"So what do you think happened?" Court asked.

"Don't know yet," Tom said, "but what if Eric had something to do with his sister's accident? What if he was strung out, maybe out of cash and looking for a fix. He goes over to his sister's house to ask for money."

"The husband made it sound like her walking the dog around that time was a routine," Mel said. "Maybe he thought she wouldn't be there and he was going to steal something."

"But Rachel's there after all, and she confronts him about his drug problem," Tom riffed. "Sounds like everybody in the family was well-versed in Eric's addiction and they wanted him to get better, but sometimes you just can't reason with a junkie. Things get ugly, he hurts her—maybe it's an accident, maybe not—then runs off to his dealer."

"Maybe he felt bad about hurting her," Court added, timid at first and then gaining steam when she realized

Tom didn't mind the spitballing. "He might even have thought she was dead when he left the house."

"Someone who's been addicted to narcotics for that long has almost got to have a history of depression along with it," Mel said. "What if he felt guilty about hurting Rachel and he intentionally overdosed?"

"We don't know yet if he overdosed," Tom reminded them. "We're still waiting on the toxicology reports, should come in later this week."

"But even if it was an overdose, who set the fire?" Court asked. "Who tried to get rid of his body?"

"Whoever he was with when he died," Mel said.

"Million-dollar question," Tom added.

CHAPTER TWELVE
COURT

"Will you tell me about your mom?" Mel asked.

It was four a.m., a dead time during most overnight shifts, and Mel and Court had been chatting on a side channel off and on all night.

They'd started with much easier subjects—assessing Tom's current theory about what happened to Eric Gilles, and how awful what happened to Rachel Tucker was. They discussed the best coffee shops and all-night diners around the city, since both of them were seasoned night owls. Then they got into their favorite music genres and authors.

All of this happened in between calls, when not much was going on and they were just keeping each other company.

And the longer they talked, the deeper they delved.

Mel told Court that her dad had run out on her mom before she was even born, and her mom had left her to be raised by her grandmother when she was ten because she just couldn't handle being a single parent.

"She convinced herself she'd be a better mom if she just wasn't there," Mel said. "I'm lucky my nonna was there with open arms."

"She sounds like a hell of a woman," Court agreed. "Do you ever see your mom anymore?"

She could hear the emotion creeping up Mel's throat when she answered, "Once or twice a year, sometimes not even that much. I figure if she doesn't care to make time for me, I shouldn't care too much about her... but that's easier said than done."

"That sounds awful," Court said. "I'm sorry."

"It's fine," Mel answered, her tone immediately hardening as she swallowed back those painful emotions. That was one thing she was great at, Court was learning —she could suppress her feelings with the best of them, and that probably served her well on the job.

Court, on the other hand, still wore her heart on her sleeve. Something she'd have to work on if she wanted to be a good cop.

Later in the night, she shared with Mel how worried her dad got whenever she mentioned taking the civil service exam, and that she wanted to take it anyway because she couldn't think of any better tribute to her mother than following in her footsteps. That's how they got around to the subject of her death. She might have lived if only she'd been wearing a bulletproof vest—such a simple thing, a small decision that changed so many lives. But she was out on patrol, doing a routine inspection of the exterior of a house after someone called in a peeping Tom. There was no reason to expect the violent scene that followed.

When Mel asked about her mom, about what she was like, Court got a lump in her throat the size of a golf ball.

"She was wonderful."

Suddenly, she was thinking about being little, standing on a step-stool in the kitchen and being her mother's 'sous chef' while they cooked dinner together.

Sitting on a swing at the park, even younger, begging her mom to push her higher, higher, so she could go all the way around.

Standing with her hand on her father's shoulder as he sat at her mother's bedside after the shooting, monitors beeping and the ventilator robotically pumping air into her lungs.

Court cleared her throat and forced a smile, even though Mel couldn't see it. "I'll tell you what... I will tell you everything you want to know about my mom if you'll have breakfast with me after work. At that Sunnyside Café you mentioned?"

Mel didn't answer right away, perhaps sensing that Court didn't have the willpower to talk about her mom over the radio without tearing up. Then she said, "That sounds great. It's a date."

Court smiled again, this one less forced. "It is?"

"If you want it to be, sure."

"I do."

Then a new call came up on her computer and she

switched over to the main dispatch channel to get back to work.

Four hours later, at the end of her shift, Court got up, stretched out the kinks of sitting in the same position all night long, and practically skipped the six blocks through downtown Fox City to the Sunnyside Café. She got a booth near the big windows at the front of the restaurant and ordered a couple glasses of water and a carafe of coffee for the two of them.

Outside, the street was busy with traffic, people rushing on their way to work. The café was relatively quiet, a sit-down type of place that most people didn't have time for on a weekday morning. That suited Court just fine—she was looking forward to a cozy meal and her first official date with Mel.

While she waited, she was thinking of stories about her mom that she could share, as promised. The one about learning to cook by her side, definitely... but perhaps the hospital-centric ones at the end weren't the best first-date material.

She poured herself a cup of coffee and slowly sipped it, watching the traffic outside lessen as people got where they were going. When her cup was empty and the waitress had been around twice asking her if she was ready to order, Court checked her phone.

It was eight-thirty, and Mel was half an hour late. No texts from her, either. Court shot off a quick message: *You on your way?*

She asked the waitress for a little more time, poured herself a second cup of coffee, and waited.

No response.

Court wondered what had gone wrong... and a little part of her started to worry, imagining the worst. *It's just because you spend eight hours a night hearing about the worst day of people's lives,* she told herself. *Nothing happened to Mel.*

Then where was she?

She texted once more, and when her second cup of coffee was empty and she'd been sitting alone in the booth for over an hour, she called. But Mel didn't answer. With a stomachache composed of worry and caffeine, Court slid out of the booth, leaving a generous tip for the server who'd kept checking on her.

As she left the café, she wondered—had Mel changed her mind about Court?

CHAPTER THIRTEEN
MEL

*I*t was early afternoon, about one o'clock, and Mel was sitting in an uncomfortable, thinly padded chair at her grandmother's bedside. Nonna was resting, her eyes closed and an oxygen mask covering her nose and mouth, and Mel thought about scrolling through the Degenhart listings on eBay.

She felt guilty even thinking about it. eBay was cheating—Nonna said it took all the fun out of the hunt, and that if the universe wanted her to find a Carnival Cobalt owl, it would deliver one to her 'the right way.' But a little, nagging part of her mind kept saying, *Buy it for her now or you might not get the chance. She doesn't have to know it came from the internet.*

Mel had been parking her squad car in the deck that morning when her grandmother's nurse, Amanda, called. She'd said Nonna was having trouble catching her breath, and she'd been asking for Ernie—her husband of forty years, who'd died when Mel was eighteen. Amanda had called an ambulance, and they were taking Nonna to the hospital.

Obviously, Mel dropped everything. She didn't even bother to go inside the station to clock out. She just ran through the parking garage to her car, then peeled out of there as fast as she could.

Nonna was just being seen by the doctor when she arrived. She called Mel 'Candace'—her mother's name— and the doctor said she had a fever of a hundred and two degrees. She was wheezing, and Amanda was patting her hand, encouraging her to relax as much as she could.

"I'd like to do a CT scan of the lungs," the doctor explained as he pulled his stethoscope from his ears. "It's likely she has pneumonia, but with someone Gloria's age, and with her health complications, I want to be thorough."

"Okay, do it," Mel agreed immediately. "Nonna, they're going to take care of you, so don't worry, okay?"

"Candace, where's your little girl?" Nonna asked, her words rumbling in her throat as she attempted to speak around the fluid building up in her lungs.

Mel had no answer. She just stood there helplessly while a couple of medical assistants wheeled Nonna out of the room on the stretcher to get the CT scan. When they were alone, Amanda came and put a hand on Mel's shoulder.

"She's a tough lady," she said. "This is a setback, but she's gonna keep fighting like she always does."

"What happened?" Mel asked, furrowing her brows. "She was fine when I called last night before my shift."

"Sometimes these things come on quickly, especially in the elderly," Amanda said. "Pneumonia is a fairly common complication of chemotherapy for someone Gloria's age. I promise, I got her here the minute I knew she needed help."

Mel nodded, trying to feel all right instead of guilty. She should have been there for her. She should have been the one riding in the ambulance, not the nurse Mel paid to look after her only remaining relative.

"Hey," Amanda said, looking at her like she could read her thoughts. "This was nobody's fault."

Mel nodded again, and put her hand on top of Amanda's, giving it a quick squeeze. "Thank you. You should go home now." She looked at the time on her phone. "Your shift ended forty-five minutes ago."

Amanda shrugged. "I don't mind. You're not the only one who cares about Gloria."

So they both sat down and waited, and Amanda finally went home a little while after Nonna came back from her CT scan. The doctor confirmed his diagnosis, ordering antibiotics and a fever reducer to be given intravenously. After about an hour, the fever broke and Nonna called Mel by her name.

"You had me worried," Mel said.

"I'm not ready to leave this world yet," Nonna answered, then cracked a smile. "We've still got owls to find."

Mel told her to rest, to let the drugs and the hospital staff do their work. "I'm not going anywhere," she said, "so you just take it easy."

Nonna had drifted off, her breathing slow and rhythmic beneath an oxygen mask. Mel had stayed by her side all day, wondering how big a sin it would be to buy Degenharts on eBay, until at last she began to nod off herself.

As her eyelids grew heavy and she tried to find a workable position in the uncomfortable hospital chair, her brain listed off all her obligations for the next twenty-four hours or so.

She'd told Zara and Kelsey that she'd meet them for a late dinner—she'd have to cancel that so she could sleep instead.

She had to work tonight.

She hoped Court would be working too, a distraction and a reason to stay awake—

Court!

Mel's eyes popped open as she realized that she'd completely left her hanging this morning. They were supposed to go on their first official date, and instead, Mel had stood her up.

"Shit," she muttered.

"Hmm?" Nonna mumbled, her eyelids fluttering.

"It's nothing, Nonna," Mel said, patting her hand. "Go back to sleep."

She got up and went into the hallway, frowning when she realized this was almost definitely Court's sleeping time too. Call and potentially wake her out of a dead sleep, adding insult to injury? Or don't call and let her think Mel stood her up on purpose?

She paced a minute or two, trying to decide which

was the lesser offense. All the while, guilt—and possibly hunger—gnawed at her belly.

What was she even doing, getting involved with a cute girl from work—the chief's daughter, no less—when her grandmother, the woman who took her in when no one else wanted her, was sick and very possibly nearing the end of her life? How could she even think about splitting her time like that, taking any time at all away from Nonna while she could still be with her?

She'd been selfish, and it wasn't fair to any of them.

Mel stopped pacing and decided a text was the best compromise she could come up with.

Court, I'm so sorry about this morning. My grandmother's in the hospital with pneumonia and I just need to be with her for a while.

She hit send, wondering if she'd just broken up with Court in a text message. Were they even going out, if she'd missed their very first date? With a sigh, Mel slipped her phone into her pocket and went back into the room, slinging both legs over the wooden arm of the hospital chair and leaning her head against the back, scrunching down and preparing to nap in the most uncomfortable position ever.

"What on earth are you doing?"

Mel opened her eyes, surprised to see Nonna alert, her eyes brighter than they'd been all day. "Just trying to get comfy," she explained.

Nonna raised an eyebrow. "And how's it going?"

Mel smiled. "Not well."

"Go home, baby girl," Nonna said. "Get a good rest because I can't be up all night worrying about you being sleep deprived on the job." She stifled a cough and added, "I've got my own work to do, getting well again."

"Nonna—"

"I'm not playing," she said in that stern voice that never failed to send fear down Mel's spine when she was a kid. "Go on, girl."

Mel sighed, then untangled herself from the pretzel-like position she'd gotten into. "You're sure?"

"Yes," Nonna said. "There are plenty of people here who can look after me better than you can."

"And you'll call if you need anything?"

"Of course."

"I love you, Nonna."

"I love you too, baby girl." Mel was partway to the door when Nonna called, "Melissa?"

"Yes?"

She pushed the oxygen mask down over her chin to say, "Don't forget to live your life just because mine is ending."

Mel gave her a weak smile and a nod, and went home —reluctantly. By the time she got to her bed, though, she was aching for sleep. She'd sacrificed a lot of it over the past few days, and she was out the moment her head hit the pillow.

*W*hen she woke up eight hours later, to the ringing of her phone alarm, it felt like only minutes had passed. She turned off the alarm, then checked her messages.

There was one from Zara, answering a text that Mel had sent her earlier in the day to say she and Kelsey were sorry to hear about Gloria and they were down to reschedule dinner whenever Mel was free.

And another one from Court. All it said was, *I understand... I hope she gets better soon.*

Well, crap. That sounded like a 'thanks for playing, please don't contact me again' text if Mel ever saw one. She set the phone down, trying to put it out of her mind, and went to take a shower and get ready for work.

While she ate a quick dinner, her first meal all day, Mel called Nonna to check in. She was doing okay and the doctor said if she kept improving, she could probably go home the following morning as long as Amanda was available to keep an eye on her and administer the antibiotics. That made Mel feel a little better about going to work that night, but she reminded Nonna to call, or have someone from the hospital call, if anything —*anything*—happened and she'd drop everything and come back.

"You worry too much," Nonna told her. "I'm a seventy-two-year-old woman with ovarian cancer. Things are going to happen, and I'll get through them until it's time for me not to."

"I wish I could be as Zen about you dying as you are," Mel told her.

"I've had a lot of time to come to terms with it," Nonna said. "You have a good night and be safe out there, okay, baby girl?"

"I will," Mel promised. She always did, even though she knew there were no guarantees in life, and there sure as hell weren't guarantees in police work.

She was still thinking about her grandmother when she pulled into the police parking deck, caught up in her own head for the last few minutes before she would need to turn that part of her brain off for the night. While she walked to the elevators, she was wondering whether, when she was Nonna's age, she would have such an enlightened view of mortality.

Probably not. Not after all the traumatic scenes and senseless violence she'd seen on the job.

Nonna was a homemaker for most of her life, a stay-at-home mom who did alterations out of her house to bring in extra money, then took on more work after her husband died just to keep herself busy. What did she know about how ugly the world could be?

"Hey... Mel!"

She turned when she heard her name, and the next thing she knew, someone was barreling into her, arms wrapping around her and blonde hair flying in her face.

"Court," she said, surprised.

Before she could even catch her breath, though, Court was enveloping her in a bear hug that felt so good, it brought tears to her eyes. She said, "I'm so sorry your grandma is in the hospital. I was thinking about you two all day."

A couple of those tears spilled over Mel's cheeks, hot like she'd been holding them in for a while, and she sank into the hug. Court smelled like coconut and her body was warm and inviting, pressed fully against Mel's in a way that was so comforting she completely forgot they were standing in the middle of the police parking deck.

"Thank you," she breathed, burying her face in Court's soft hair.

They just stood like that for a long moment, in each other's arms, until at last Mel felt like she'd pulled herself together again... and also realized that if they didn't start moving toward the elevator, they'd both be late. She lifted her head and Court used her thumbs to dry the tears on her cheeks.

Then Mel said, "I'm sorry about this morning. Were you mad?"

"No," Court said, so quickly Mel actually believed it. "I figured if you didn't show up, you had a good reason. I'm just sorry it was your nonna. How's she doing?"

"Much better now," Mel said. She slipped her hand into Court's and they walked over to the elevator while she filled her in on the last twelve hours.

Maybe Nonna was right. Maybe she *did* need to live her life, because once the shock of Amanda's call had worn off and Nonna was out of the woods, all Mel could think about was Court and how much she'd missed her.

CHAPTER FOURTEEN
COURT

*C*ourt was just gathering her things at the end of her shift when Tom Logan peeked his head into the dispatchers' office.

"Hey, Wilson," he called, then waved her over.

She slung her bag over her shoulder and met him at the door, stifling a yawn. "Morning, Tom, what's going on?"

"I just got a call on my way into the precinct," he said. "Rachel Tucker is awake. I need to get down to the hospital and interview her—want to tag along?"

Court was instantly awake at the promise of more hands-on policework. It was better than a shot of espresso. "Hell yes. Did you talk to Mel yet?"

"Nah, came here first because it was on the way to my desk," he said. "You want to call her?"

"Sure."

Court had been texting Mel off and on all night, and they'd had a few quick side-channel conversations when things were slow. She'd mostly just been trying to comfort her and keep her mind off her grandmother's pneumonia, and she wasn't even sure Mel would want to come along this morning. But, selfishly, Court wanted to see her again, so she called her cell while they walked to Tom's desk so he could pick up the Eric Gilles file.

"Hey, how are you feeling?" Court asked as soon as Mel picked up.

"Tired," Mel admitted. "And at the same time, a little too wired to sleep. I know Nonna's out of the woods now but I hate that she's still at the hospital. I may have had a couple of energy drinks last night in a misguided attempt to focus on other things."

"She'll be okay," Court said, wishing she had the authority to truly mean that. "Hey, are you up for a little more policework this morning? Rachel's awake and Tom wants to go to the hospital to talk to her."

There was a little hesitation on Mel's end of the line, then she said, "Actually, that'd work out well. Nonna's at Fox County too, and I wanted to stop by and see how she's doing this morning. I'll just drive over separately so I can visit her after we're done with Rachel."

Court hung up a minute or two later, after shamelessly begging a ride off of Mel purely so they could spend a little more time together. Tom looked up from his computer, where he was checking his email.

"She coming?"

"Yeah, she'll meet us in the parking garage and I'm going to ride with her."

"Oh, you don't like my driving, huh?"

Court just shrugged, and Tom didn't look all that offended. Then he pointed to his email.

"Got a message from the Medical Examiner's Office," he said. "Toxicology confirms that Gilles was under the influence the night he died. They found both heroin and cocaine in his system. A lot of both, but the chemist says that for a long-term addict, there's no real way to know if they were lethal levels."

"So he was dead before the fire was lit, but we still don't know if he died of an overdose," Court said, pensive. "We don't know much of anything, do we?"

Tom shrugged. "Give it time. Some cases are harder than others."

Court met up with Mel in the parking garage and had a strong urge to pull Mel into a hug again—her body felt so nice and Court was really beginning to crave that vanilla-clove scent of hers. Plus, Mel just looked like she could really use another good bear hug.

But Tom was standing nearby, so instead, Court waited til they got inside Mel's car, then reached across the center console to take her hand.

"I missed you."

"I missed you too," Mel said.

They held hands all the way to the hospital, and Court distracted Mel from her Nonna troubles by giving her the latest details on the case. They kept stealing furtive glances at each other all the way to the ICU, and it felt like falling in love, the way Court's heart skipped a beat every time Mel's eyes met her own and the constant urge to be with her, close to her.

It was wonderful, and unexpected.

But when the elevator came to a stop at the ICU and the doors slid open, they both had to put their game faces on and focus on the case.

Tom flashed his badge at the nurses' station and told the woman there that Rachel Tucker's family was expecting them. He barely even slowed down now that they knew the way, marching right past the nurse and down the hall full of beeping monitors.

Things were a little more optimistic today, though, because this time, Rachel wasn't lying inert in her hospital bed, wires coming off her in half a dozen directions. She was sitting up, eyes open albeit a little glassy, working on a boxed juice while her husband and mother sat at her bedside and kept her company.

Tom knocked on the doorframe. "Good morning."

Rachel's brow furrowed slightly, and Adam reached a hand out to touch his wife's shoulder. "These are the police we told you about. They're trying to figure out what happened to Eric?"

Rachel's eyes went even glassier, and a jolt of pain registered in her face, like she'd gotten an electric shock. The poor woman had just come out of a coma, and now she was having to deal with the fact that her brother was dead. Court had a strong urge to flee back to her safe little place in the dispatch office, to admit that maybe she didn't have what it took to deal with awful situations like this after all.

But she was here now, and all she had to do was stand and listen.

"Is this a good time?" Tom asked.

Rachel nodded, and her mother, Lydia, waved them into the room. "Good a time as any, I guess."

Court and Mel stood just inside the door, and Tom stood at the foot of the bed. He took out the small notebook he always kept in his pocket, then asked, "How are you feeling, Rachel?"

"Like I got hit by a bus," she said, her voice a little scratchy. She gave up on the juice box and just sat back in the bed. Her head was still bandaged, but it looked like someone had done their best to wash her hair since the last time Court saw her.

"Can you tell me what happened to you?" Tom prompted.

"I told you last time, she fell," Adam said. He sounded a little testy, understandable considering everything that had happened to his family in the past week. Still, combative family members never made things easy—Court knew that much just from working the phones.

Tom smiled politely as he said, "Perhaps you and Ms. Gilles can step out for a moment, get yourselves some coffee?"

Adam grunted, but he squeezed Rachel's shoulder one more time and told her they'd be right back. He and Lydia left the small room, and suddenly there was a whole lot more air to go around.

Tom took Lydia's seat beside the bed. "I'm sorry, Rachel, I promise we'll keep this short. I just need to hear what happened from you."

"You don't think Adam did this, do you?" she asked. "Because he would never hurt me."

"No," Tom reassured her. "We're here about your brother. I had an inkling that maybe you saw him the day of your accident, before you fell. It's awfully coincidental timing, you see what I'm saying?"

Rachel just studied him for a moment, then looked to Court and Mel, trying to be as unobtrusive as possible by the door. Then she turned back to Tom.

"I did see him," she said. "That afternoon."

"Eric?"

"Yes. I was walking the dog and when I got home, he was sitting on the stoop."

"Alone?"

"Yes."

"And did you let him inside the house?" Tom asked.

Rachel nodded, then winced as if the slight movement hurt her injured head. "We went into the kitchen. I needed to get Max some water."

"Max?"

"Our puppy."

"Right," Tom said, jotting the name down just to keep everything straight. "And what was Eric doing at your house?"

She averted her eyes, stared at the juice box. For a minute, Court didn't think she would answer at all, but Tom just waited her out and at last she said, "He was upset. And high."

"Your mother mentioned his addiction struggles," Tom said. "Had he been using again for some time?"

Rachel shook her head. "No, he was doing really well, actually. We were all so proud of him, it's been such a constant demon of his."

"Any idea what set off the relapse?"

Rachel picked up the juice box, picking at a fold in the cardboard. "No."

Tom waited again, but this time, nothing more came. So he said, "You mentioned he was upset. What about?"

"I wanted him to go to rehab," she said. "We all did—it's worked for him in the past. But he just wanted money. He said he needed to pay his utility bill but I knew he was just going to buy more drugs."

"And did you give him any money?"

She shook her head.

"Did he attempt to steal from you then?"

Again, Rachel just shook her head, eyes still fixed on her juice box.

"Rachel..." Tom waited until she met his gaze, then he asked gently, "Did you and Eric get in a physical altercation that afternoon? Was he the one who hurt you?"

Now her brow creased with anger and she set the juice box down on the tray table so hard that a few drops of orange liquid splattered on the surface.

"No," she said. "Eric didn't hurt me, he's never hurt me, and neither has Adam. I tripped over my dog's leash after Eric left—it was a dumb, clumsy thing to do and I was distracted because my brother was using again, but it was just an accident."

"Okay," Tom said, his voice soft and placating.

But Rachel was angry now. "Is that all you need from

me? Because I think my family's been through enough without detectives nosing around, blaming people for things that just *happened*. It's *awful*."

Just then, Adam and Lydia came back into the room, both of them going defensively to Rachel's bedside. Neither of them had coffee in their hands and Court figured they'd just been standing in the hallway the whole time, waiting for their chance to return.

"I'm sorry to have disturbed you," Tom said, getting out of the chair. He was being deferential, but he also made a point to say, "We'll be in touch if we have any further questions."

Lydia swooped right in and took her seat back, and none of them looked at Tom, Court or Mel as they saw themselves out. As soon as they got to the hallway, Tom gave the two of them a wide-eyed look, blowing out a breath and shaking his head.

"Defensive much?" he said in a whisper.

CHAPTER FIFTEEN
MEL

*T*hey managed to stay quiet until they got to the elevators. When the doors had slid shut, though, Tom asked, "Thoughts?"

"She did seem defensive, especially toward the end," Court said. "I'm sure she's processing a lot right now though, having just woken up from a serious head injury only to find out her brother is dead."

"She was evasive too, though," Mel added. "Did you notice how fidgety she was when she was telling Tom her version of events? She kept picking at her juice box."

Tom nodded. "Good. So, do we believe her?"

Mel could see the way Court puffed out her chest, obviously proud that Tom was letting the two of them have a real say in the case—if only during the brainstorming parts of it.

"I do," she said. "Everything she told us today matches with what Adam and Lydia have told us in the past week."

She looked to Mel, who couldn't bring herself to be enthusiastically pro-Rachel. "I dunno... Aside from the fidgeting, she was convincing, I'll give her that. But I just keep coming back to how convenient all this is. Her brother dies and his body is burned on the same day she accidentally trips over her dog's leash and hits her head so hard she goes into a coma?"

Tom grunted. "Gotta agree with you there. I've been at this a long time and I don't see too many genuine coincidences in homicide investigation."

"So what do you think happened?" Court asked just as the elevator came to a stop again on the floor where the hospital was keeping Nonna for observation.

"This is my floor," Mel pointed out.

"Come on," Court said, stepping off the elevator with her and tugging Tom by his shirtsleeve. Mel almost laughed—only the chief's daughter could get away with a move like that—but Tom made no objection as he followed them into the small lobby just outside the elevators.

There was a vending machine in one corner, and Tom went over to buy everyone a round of sodas while they finished their assessment of Rachel Tucker's story. He cracked open a Dr Pepper and said, "I don't know what happened yet—I try not to pigeonhole myself into any theories too early in a case. But I do think that Rachel's keeping something from us, probably something about Eric's visit that she doesn't want her husband or her mom to find out about."

"Like maybe she really did give him money for drugs?" Mel wondered.

"Or maybe the argument they had was bigger than she let on," Tom answered. "What if they really got into it and things got physical? What if Eric tripped her, or pushed her?"

"A loving sister wouldn't want anyone's last memory of her brother to be a violent one," Court said.

"So let's say Eric hurt her, then what?" Tom asked.

Mel thought for a minute, her mind running through all the drug-motivated crimes she'd responded to over the years. A lot of them involved robberies, petty theft, commonly from family members and close friends.

"Maybe he felt bad about it, but not bad enough to stay. Maybe he underestimated how bad she was hurt, or freaked out and left before he could see she needed help," she thought aloud. "Or maybe he knew exactly what he'd done to his sister and he went off to get high as a way of forgetting the guilt, and ended up OD'ing."

"Was Rachel robbed?" Mel asked Tom.

He shook his head. "Not that anybody's admitting to, but you could be right—families make excuses for the addicts in their lives all the time, not wanting to get them in trouble or else not wanting to push them away."

"But even if that's how Rachel got hurt, and it explains the drugs in Eric's system at his time of death," Court said, "who drove his car out to the middle of nowhere and set it on fire?"

"That," Tom answered, "is what we have to find out next."

He chugged the rest of his Dr Pepper, then crumpled the can and tossed it into a recycling bin near the vending machines.

"I gotta get back to the station, take care of some paperwork junk," he said. He turned to Court. "You riding with me or sticking with Pine?"

Court looked from Tom to Mel, and Mel felt a little twinge of guilt in her stomach. This was just supposed to be a quick detour on her way to visit Nonna, but a part of her wanted to stay with Court, to insulate herself from her problems the same way Eric Gilles numbed his problems with drugs.

No. Nonna needed her.

"I'm sorry, Court," she said. "You better get a ride with Tom because I'm not sure how long I'm going to be here. I might even be able to bring Nonna home this afternoon if the doctor releases her."

"No, it's fine," Court said, an understanding look on her face. "Tell your grandmother I hope she's feeling better, and you know you can call me if you need any help, right?"

Mel smiled. "Thanks. But Nonna's got in-home nurses I can call to help out if she ends up getting released today. I'll tell her you said hi."

"Word to your grandmother," Tom said, completely straight-faced, and Mel had to twist her lips up to keep from laughing.

"Does that mean you want me to say hi for you too?"

"Sure," he said. "Whatever kids these days are saying in these situations."

"Lord," Court said, shaking her head and chuckling. "Let's get you back to the precinct where you can't embarrass yourself." Tom punched the elevator button, and then just as the doors were opening, Court threw her arms around Mel and gave her a kiss on the cheek. "See you later, cutie."

They both disappeared into the elevator, and Mel walked dreamily up the hall, entirely too happy for a person going to visit their sickly grandmother.

CHAPTER SIXTEEN
COURT

*C*ourt met Mel at the police station that evening, just as they were both clocking in for their shifts. She looked worn out, like she hadn't gotten much sleep, and Court let her go first at the time clock.

"How's Nonna doing?" she asked while Mel punched in.

"Good," she said. "Still has pneumonia, but they gave her a few breathing treatments at the hospital and said she was well enough to go home again. Amanda and I spent most of the morning getting her situated and making sure she had everything she needed to be comfortable."

"You seem like a really good granddaughter," Court said. Mel stepped aside so she could have her turn at the time clock, and Court brushed her hand covertly over Mel's as she passed her.

"Anything else happen on the Gilles case after we parted ways?" Mel asked.

Court shook her head. "Nothing important. The body was released to the funeral home, though. Dr. Trace said there was nothing further for the medical examiner's office to do, so the family will be able to have a funeral."

"That's good," Mel said. "They can get some closure now."

"I don't know how much closure you can get during an open homicide investigation," Court said with a small grunt.

She was thinking about her mother's funeral, how there were so many roses they made the entire room reek, how the smell nauseated her to this day. There was no question about who had killed her, but that didn't make things any easier. The funeral was still one of the worst days of her life.

"Whoever invented the concept of closure clearly never lost anyone close to them."

"I'm sorry," Mel said. "I wasn't thinking–"

Court waved her hand, forcing the emotions back down. "No, no, it's fine. I didn't mean to go to an ugly place like that." She checked the time on the clock again, then said, "I have to get to my computer and log in or I'll get in trouble... Walk me to dispatch?"

"Sure," Mel said.

They took the stairs, holding hands when they were sure there was no one else around to see them. Court would have held Mel's hand everywhere, no matter what, but then, she was the chief's daughter and nobody dared to judge her to her face. Mel didn't have that luxury, and she still needed to worry about being taken seriously, especially as both a female officer and a queer woman.

So when they got up to the third floor, Court gave Mel's hand a little squeeze, then let it go. They walked to the door of the dispatch office, and Court paused outside of it. She had just a couple minutes to log in before she was officially late for her shift, but she was willing to risk it.

"The funeral is on Friday," she said. "I asked Tom if he was going to go to the calling hours, scope things out a bit, but he said detectives don't do that kind of thing unless they have a really good reason. He *didn't* say that I couldn't go, though, and I'm thinking about it."

"To scope things out?" Mel asked.

Court shrugged. "That, and also to pay my respects. This is the first case I've been allowed to really get involved in, and I feel sort of connected to Eric Gilles."

Mel nodded. "I understand that. I remember some of the people I've interacted with on patrol more than others. You don't think that the family will mind?"

A small smile broke involuntarily across Court's lips as she admitted, "I was planning to go in disguise. And I was wondering... I know this is not great timing because of your grandma and everything, but... do you want to come with?"

Now Mel was smiling too. "In disguise? What kind?"

Court rolled her eyes. "I mean, I'm not planning on going as the Hamburglar or anything. But I figured I could get glasses and a short wig... and I bet you'd make a cute icy blonde."

Mel laughed. "I don't know about all that... but I'll go with you, as long as it's just to pay our respects."

Court nodded eagerly. "Discreetly, from a distance."

"Hey, you better get in there," Mel said, checking the time on her phone.

"Damn," Court said. It was so easy to lose track of time when she was with Mel because nothing else seemed to matter when she was around. "Be safe out there tonight."

"I will," Mel promised. "Have a good night."

She headed back for the stairwell and Court lingered in the hallway for just a few seconds longer, enjoying the view.

***

The funeral home was packed when Court and Mel arrived on Friday morning at the beginning of calling hours. There were clearly a lot of people who cared about Eric Gilles, which must have been a comfort to his family, but it was also convenient for Court and Mel—it made the job of blending in much easier. Especially since Mel had nixed the disguise idea.

An hour ago, they'd been standing in front of the full-length mirror in Mel's bathroom, a white-blonde wig on Mel's head and a skeptical look on her face. "You seriously want me to wear this?"

"It's cute," Court had answered, running her fingers through the synthetic strands to tidy the blunt-cut bob. "You look great."

"Great and inconspicuous are two very different things," Mel had pointed out.

"Oh, fine," Court had said, pulling the wig off Mel's head. "You're right... but you're keeping the wig and we're going to go out sometime and have fun in disguise."

Mel had laughed at that, then set about styling her natural hair into something that was much more funeral-appropriate. She'd toned down Court's get-up too, only letting her keep the thick-framed glasses she'd chosen. By the time they finally left the apartment, Mel's bedroom and bathroom looked like a tornado had devastated them, and they'd both settled on demure, forgettable black slacks. Mel was in a slate-gray collared shirt, and Court wore a black silk blouse with delicate white flowers printed on it.

They looked around the viewing room now, and Court asked, "Should we get in the receiving line?"

"Umm, not unless you actually want to come face-to-face with the people you were trying to disguise yourself from," Mel pointed out.

The line stretched nearly to the door, with dozens of people lined up to file past the closed casket and give their condolences to Eric's immediate family. There were a lot of service men and women in their dress uniforms. Adam was standing at attention in his Army Service Uniform beside Rachel, who was looking tired and sitting in a wheelchair.

"Mm, yeah, probably best not to get *that* involved today," Court agreed.

"Let's just stand near the guest book," Mel suggested.

"There are a lot of people there so we can observe unnoticed."

They did their best to fade into the crowd. Court scanned the guest book when no one was using it, although she didn't see any names of note there, and they watched the receiving line continually flow through the room.

Court and Mel shared a moment of silence among themselves in lieu of actually speaking to the family, and Court sent a prayer into the universe that Tom would find out what happened to Eric Gilles and who tried to get rid of his body, and that the person would be justly punished.

She was absorbed in her own thoughts when Mel nudged her with her elbow and whispered, "Check it out."

She nodded in the family's direction, and Court saw that Adam was talking to someone in a high and tight haircut like his own. The expression on Adam's face was tense, even from across the room, and not the kind of tense that results from several hours of standing still and receiving condolences.

"He looks on edge," Mel whispered.

"Can you hear what they're saying?" Court asked.

Mel shook her head. "Too far away."

"Somebody from the dark side of Eric's life?" Court theorized. "An addict too, who they wouldn't want at his calling hours?"

Mel chewed on her lower lip, then shook her head

again when the man turned away from Adam. "Look at the buzz cut—I bet he's ex-military. I doubt he's another heroin addict."

"Eric was," Court pointed out. "Maybe this guy was his hook-up? That would explain why Adam's so unhappy to see him."

"Anything's possible," Mel conceded. "But why would he come to the funeral?"

*T*he man got out of line and started to head for the door. Court and Mel, standing near it, averted their eyes and pretended to be deeply absorbed in the prayer cards they'd picked up near the guest book. He marched past them. He had salt and pepper in his beard and crow's feet at the corners of his eyes, but his posture was still perfectly rigid and military-precise.

Court had to admit that nothing about him screamed *drug addict,* but then, a lot of functional addicts were experts at hiding their problems.

When he was gone, Court looked back toward Adam, who'd moved on to the next person in line. Lydia, standing on the other side of Rachel's wheelchair, looked exhausted, and Court wondered how much sleep she'd gotten in the past week. Probably not much.

Her own dad barely slept at all for weeks after her mom passed, and she'd had to practically drag him off the couch and shove him down the hall to make him at least lie down. With Rachel's injury taking up everyone's spare energy, Lydia probably didn't have anyone in her life who could do that for her.

"Well, should we get out of here before we're spotted?" Court asked.

"Yeah, let's go," Mel said, holding out her arm. Court slipped her hand into the crook of her elbow and they headed for the door. "Do you want to get some food before it's time for bed?"

"You saying you want to 'buy me dinner first'?" Court asked with a smirk. "Yeah, I'm famished."

They were at Mel's car when the door to the funeral home opened again, more forcefully than necessary. Mel was just sitting down behind the wheel, but Court crouched on the passenger side, peeking over the roof and hoping not to be spotted as she watched Lydia burst onto the steps looking fiercer than Court had ever seen her. On her heels was a younger woman in expensive-looking stilettos and a burgundy dress, and they were talking so loud their voices carried across the parking lot.

"...can't believe you would show up like this," Lydia was saying.

"Hey, what's going on?" Mel asked, leaning across the inside of the car to talk to Court.

"Argument," she said, quietly so they wouldn't notice that they were being watched. "Eric's mom and a woman I don't recognize. Come here."

She opened the passenger door and Mel scooched across the car and climbed out to crouch beside Court. "Wouldn't it be awkward if they caught us peeping like this?" she whispered.

"Shh," Court said, bumping into Mel with her shoulder. They stayed pressed together, just the tops of their heads peeking over Mel's car.

"I'm his wife," the woman in burgundy was saying. "I think I have a right to be here."

"You haven't been his wife in years, Vee, not in any way other than legally," Lydia shot back. "You're not fooling anyone—we all know what you're doing here in that strumpet dress. Who wears red to a funeral?"

"It's a perfectly reasonable–" the woman apparently named Vee started to say, then huffed in frustration and started over. "What do you mean, you know what I'm doing here?"

"Don't pretend you're not getting impatient to get your hands on Eric's pension," Lydia hissed. "I know you never divorced him because you wanted that money."

"I never divorced him because he was always too strung out to show up to court!" Vee spat back. "It had nothing to do with his pension!"

"Oh, so you're going to refuse that money?" Lydia baited her. "You're going to tell the military that the money should go to his grieving mother and sister instead of you?"

Vee turned red in the face, nearly matching her dress, but she didn't speak.

Lydia put a hand behind her ear. "What's that? You can't even pretend you're going to do the right thing."

"What's the right thing?" Vee asked. "Is it struggling through *years* of addiction counseling and Narcotics Anonymous meetings and breakdowns and relapses? Is it standing by someone I loved for far longer than any sane person would? I'm sorry if I think I'm entitled to a little bit of compensation for all the shit Eric put me through, Lydia. The pension's not even that big."

Lydia just snorted. "Tell that to your Jimmy Choos."

Vee crossed her arms in front of herself and looked down at her feet. "They're second-hand."

"Still," Lydia grumbled, almost too softly to be audible from Court and Mel's vantage point. She took a step back toward the door, then pointed her finger at Vee. "You stay away from my family. If you really wanted to do the right thing, you wouldn't have given up on my son. The rest of us sure as hell don't need you now."

She spun on her heels—sensible black flats in contrast to Vee's stilettos—and went back inside the funeral home without another word. Vee stayed on the steps for a minute, her hands balled into fists, then she stomped into the parking lot, away from Mel's car.

She took a couple of steps and fell off one heel, rolling her ankle. "Fuck!" she shouted, then fumbled at the buckles until she had the stilettos off her feet. She walked barefoot over to a twenty-year-old Mercedes Benz, got in, and roared out of the parking lot.

When she was gone, Court and Mel stood upright, letting out a tense breath.

"Well, there's a woman with champagne tastes and a caviar budget," Mel said. "Should we tell Tom about her?"

Court nodded. "I'm sure the estranged wife was

already on his list of people to contact, but I don't think he has yet. Sounds like there's motive, though."

"Sounds like she's got an ax to grind, too," Mel added. She walked back around to the driver's side, saying, "Come on—let's eat."

CHAPTER SEVENTEEN
MEL

*T*hey found a burger place not too far from the funeral home and, over fries and shakes, they discussed Lydia's blow-out with her son's estranged wife. Court asked about Nonna and Mel said she was doing much better.

"Are you gonna go see her again before work tonight?" Court asked, reaching across the table to steal one of Mel's fries just because she could.

Mel swatted at her hand. "You have your own."

Court flashed her a smile. "Yours just look so tempting."

Damn, this woman knew how to get exactly what she wanted. Mel nudged her plate closer to the center of the table and let Court snatch another fry, even though they both knew this wasn't about delicious fried, salty potatoes.

Court's foot brushed up against Mel's beneath the table as she answered, "I'm off tomorrow, thankfully. I'm planning to sleep for about eighteen hours to catch up, but I'll probably go over to Nonna's house in the afternoon tomorrow... maybe see if she's up for a quick spin through the flea market as long as the weather's nice."

"Still hunting the elusive Carnival Cobalt owl, huh?"

Mel smiled. "You remembered."

"Of course," Court said, biting into one of her own fries with a satisfied look. "And the other one you mentioned was..." She thought for a second, a charming dimple appearing in her cheek, then said, "Custard Cream?"

"Custard Opal," Mel said. "But that was damn close."

"Well, I'm a good listener," Court said.

"That'll serve you well as a police officer," Mel pointed out. "Have you signed up to take the civil service exam yet?"

Court looked down at her plate, suddenly bashful. This was quite possibly the only subject that she didn't ooze confidence over, and Mel knew it had to do with her dad.

"I will," she promised. "Not this time around... maybe next time they offer it."

Mel decided not to push her. They'd already had an eventful morning, and she knew she was feeling tired. Court probably was too, and that was no time to pester someone on a sensitive subject. So instead, she picked up Court's milkshake—chocolate to Mel's strawberry—and took a sip, then asked, "So, what did you think of my apartment?"

That confidence bounced right back. With a sly look on her face, Court said, "I wish we could have stayed longer."

"You'll have to come back sometime," Mel said. "I'll give you the grand tour."

There really wasn't much that Court hadn't already seen. Mel lived in a one-bedroom that was perfect for her, but nothing to brag about, and Court had already been in the living room, the bedroom and the bathroom. All that was left to see was the kitchen... but they weren't *really* talking about the apartment.

Court stole her milkshake back, and Mel let her eyes linger on her, watching her lips purse around the straw as she took a sip.

She was gorgeous, and fun, and sexy, and Mel's heart galloped every time she was around her. She just had to make sure she was spending time with Court for the right reasons, and not just because she provided a welcome distraction when Mel really should have been there for her grandmother instead.

---

*S*he spent most of her day off dead to the world, emerging from her bedroom in the late after-noon with pillow marks on her cheek. She touched base with Zara and Kelsey so they would know she was still alive, promising to get dinner with them soon, then went over to Nonna's house to see how she was doing.

Mel found her sitting in her overstuffed recliner with

a humidifier running on the side table next to her and a cup of tea in hand.

"Looks like Amanda's got you all hooked up, huh?"

Nonna nodded. "She made me chicken noodle soup too. There's leftovers in the fridge if you want some."

Mel helped herself—Amanda was a great cook and Mel pretty much never turned down an opportunity for a hot meal that she didn't have to cook herself. She and Nonna chatted for a while, and they watched a little TV together—Nonna had gotten hooked on reruns of *This is Us* thanks to some of the nurses at the hospital. Mel didn't really feel like sobbing over sappy television shows before work, so she was sort of glad when the night nurse arrived and gave Mel an excuse to leave.

That night when she got to the precinct, she had a Thermos full of chicken noodle soup and a head full of TV drama. She hung around the time clock for a few minutes, hoping to run into Court, but had no luck. So instead, she punched in then headed back down to the parking garage to pick up her squad car.

She was just getting comfortable and adjusting the seat how she liked it when her phone chimed from its spot on the passenger seat. It was Court.

Hey, sorry I missed you at the time clock... I kinda like our pre-shift rendezvous.

Mel smiled to herself. She liked them too. She wrote back, *I missed you too. Running late?*

Sort of. I was here, but Tom called and distracted me. Dr. Trace filed Gilles' case as an undetermined death.

Mel frowned. She typed, *What does that mean?*

She couldn't determine cause or manner of death based on the autopsy and lab work. Tom says now it's up to him to find evidence that proves it's a homicide. If not that, there'll at least be desecration and arson charges.

Mel wrote back, *Did you tell him about the ex-wife?* She wished they could have had this conversation in person. It'd go so much faster, and then she'd get the benefit of seeing the nuances of Court's expressions.

Yeah. He didn't seem super concerned, said funerals are high-tension times even in ordinary circumstances, but he said he'd look into it.

Mel sighed, then told Court she had to go on active duty and start her patrol. Court told her to be safe, then Mel radioed in to let the dispatchers know she was available.

The first part of her shift was pretty dull. She took her usual route, stopped off to get coffee around two a.m., and made a few routine traffic stops. It would have been a completely unremarkable night if not for one call in particular.

A little after six a.m., when the sky was just beginning to lighten and the sun wasn't quite up yet, Court came on the radio saying, "We've got a 10-54 at UStore Self-Storage on Cabot Avenue. Car 34, are you available?"

Mel sat up a little straighter, alert and ready. A 10-54 was a possible dead body, and at a storage unit. Not your standard overnight call. She picked up her radio. "I'm about five minutes away. Proceeding there now."

"Copy, Car 34," Court said. "Sending an additional unit your way."

She pulled into a nearby gas station and used the lot to turn around, accelerating through the quiet streets. She found the storage facility easily enough—it was one of those places that pop up in rough neighborhoods, painted bright orange for visibility. She'd seen billboards advertising it before, though she'd never responded to a scene there.

Inside, the place was like a maze. All the storage units were accessible from the outdoors, like a single-story motel made of row upon row of units with orange-painted roll-up doors.

After driving slowly past the first two rows, Mel spotted a man waving her down. She turned down that row and the man squinted, holding up a hand to shield his eyes from her headlights. She was the first on the scene.

She parked and turned on her body cam, leaving the squad car running as she stepped out. "Morning, sir, I'm Officer Pine."

Before she got any further than that, the man

demanded, "Do the police clean up crime scenes or do I gotta hire a guy to do that?"

Oh boy... this was going to be a messy one.

"Well, let's just see what's going on first," Mel said. The truth was that she could smell the sweet, sickening odor of decay already and this man was definitely going to need the services of a biohazard clean-up crew... but she didn't want to get ahead of herself. "Can I get your name, please?"

"Cripes, I know I'm gonna have to pay for this out of my own pocket," he went on. "This is what I get for trying to run a business."

"You own the storage facility?"

"Yeah, unfortunately," he said. "Name's Sam Burns."

"Thank you, sir," Mel said, jotting his name down in her notepad. "And what is it that you found here?"

She knew she was going to have to go inside the unit and have a look for herself. That smell was not making her particularly eager, though, and without backup, she needed to know what to expect.

"Just go look—you'll see for yourself the minute you raise the door," Sam said, looking nauseated.

Well, that was no help. She decided to stall until the second officer arrived. "Do you have the name and contact information of the renter?"

"Mm-hmm," he grunted, reaching into his back pocket for his phone. "Knew you'd need that so I pulled it up while I was waiting... while I wasn't dry-heaving, that is."

Mel ignored that last comment and jotted down the

information he showed her. *Eddie Banks*. She was squinting at the screen, trying to read the rental agreement that Sam had pulled up for her, when she heard the single *wop* of a police car alerting them that backup had arrived.

Thank God.

While she waited for the other officer to park behind her and get situated, she asked Sam, "When was the unit rented?"

"'Bout three months ago," he said. "Never had a problem, he paid on time, and then last week the people who rent the unit right next door started complaining about a smell. They come out here a lot—they're flea market people and they store their stuff here on off days. I come out this morning cuz I couldn't sleep, figured I might as well get a jump on the day. Now I wish I hadn't."

Now he was being a chatterbox.

Mel jotted down everything she thought might be relevant, and by the time she was done, the second officer was walking up to them. It was a guy she knew well from the night shift—Luis Rodriguez. He was in his mid-forties, a little bit soft around the spare tire area but Mel had never seen him at a scene he couldn't handle. That was good news, at least.

He introduced himself to Sam. Mel gave him a quick rundown, then they told Sam to hang back by the squad cars while they investigated. Mel and Luis walked over to the storage unit, pulling their flashlights out of their utility belts.

"Is it just me," Luis whispered, "or are you getting a *Silence of the Lambs* vibe?"

"If that door doesn't open all the way, I am not crawling under it like Clarice Starling," Mel warned him.

It did open, though, and Mel had to struggle to keep from staggering backward as the smell assaulted her.

"Good Christ!" Luis said what she was thinking. After her eyes adjusted to the dark within the unit and her stomach decided, thankfully, not to revolt, Mel saw the source.

There was a couch in the middle of the unit, and on top of it lay a woman, bloated and decomposing after days or even weeks inside a hot metal storage unit. Mel swept her flashlight around just enough to verify that there was no one else in the unit, then she retreated to her squad car to call it in.

"Dispatch, this is Car 34 at the UStore," she said, taking deep breaths of clean air while she could. "We've definitely got a body. Going to need the medical examiner out here."

"Do you need me for anything else?" Sam asked as soon as she put down the radio. He was looking decidedly green.

Mel looked to Luis, deferring to his seniority. He shook his head. "As long as we know how to contact you —" Mel nodded, she'd gotten all that information. "— we'll be in touch."

"Okay, good," Sam said. "I'm just gonna go to the office at the front of the lot and puke for a while."

He walked away holding his stomach, and when he

was out of earshot, Mel nodded toward the unit and asked, "What do you make of that?"

"Did you notice the bucket with a toilet seat on it in the corner?"

She shook her head, embarrassed to say that this scene had gotten to her and she hadn't noticed much of anything before she fled back to the safety of her car.

"Could be indigent," Luis said. "Maybe she was living in the unit, overdosed or something while she was in there."

"The owner showed me the rental agreement. There's a man's name on the form," Mel pointed out.

Luis shrugged. "Could be foul play then."

"I just can't believe nobody found her until now," Mel said, still sucking in fresh air like she might never get it again. "She had to be decomposing in there for a while."

CHAPTER EIGHTEEN

COURT

"So that kind of stuff doesn't bother you at all?"

Court was curled up on Mel's couch, sipping a cup of decaf and pumping her for details about the storage unit scene. Mel sat beside her, hair wet and wrapped up after a shower, smelling like warm vanilla and rich cloves and making Court want to lunge across the couch at her.

She'd wanted to hear about the scene—it sounded even more gritty and interesting than the car fire that had initially brought them together. But she also wanted to take Mel up on her 'apartment tour' offer.

Not that they'd done much touring so far. As soon as they plopped down on the couch with their coffee mugs, Court had pulled Mel's legs across her lap under the guise of letting her stretch out, and now she was exactly where she wanted to be.

Mel shook her head. "Not really, aside from the smell. You should have seen what my old partner, Zara, was like at crime scenes, though. She would have thrown up at this one for sure."

Court laughed. "I probably would have too."

"You get used to it," Mel said. "Maybe it isn't something anyone *should* get used to... but when you've been a cop for a while, it's just inevitable. You see some crazy shit out there."

"Is Zara used to it now?" Court asked.

Mel smirked. "She found a loophole—transferred to narcotics so now she rarely encounters gruesome scenes like that."

"You said it seemed likely that drugs were involved in this case, though," Court said. She really wished she could have been there with Mel, actually seen it first-hand, and she wondered what that said about her.

"Yeah, the investigator from the medical examiner's office found a used needle in between the couch cushions," Mel said. "It's very likely she died of an overdose."

"So much of that happening in this city," Court said, shaking her head.

"That's why Zara went into narcotics," Mel said. She smiled. "She thinks she's going to take heroin off our streets singlehandedly, and I kinda hope she does. If anyone can, it's Zara."

"My dad's mentioned her before," Court said. "He likes her."

"What's he say about me?" Mel asked, setting her coffee down and scooting a little closer to Court.

She smiled. "As a cop, or as a person?"

"Does Chief Wilson think of me as anything other

than a cop?" Mel countered. "Heck, I'm probably flattering myself that he's even aware I exist. Fox County has a large police force."

"Oh, he knows you exist," Court said, reaching over Mel's legs to set down her own mug, then letting her hands trail over her skin and rest on her shins. "I may have mentioned you a time or two."

"Is that so?"

Court nodded. "Only terrible things though... like how you spend the whole night flirting with me..."

Mel's mouth popped open in surprise. "No."

"Oh yeah," Court said. "And how you pretend to take an interest in open investigations just to get close to me..."

Mel laughed. "You haven't really mentioned me to your dad, have you?"

Court relented. "Not like that. But I have told him about the smart, hard-working patrol officer I work with."

She ran her fingertips lightly up and down Mel's bare shin, wondering if she had the guts to inch any higher. Mel was wearing a bath robe over a pair of cotton shorts and a tank top, and Court had to work real hard to keep her eyes from roaming over her toned thighs.

"What about you?" she asked. "Have you told your grandma about the hot dispatcher you work with?"

"Well... not in so many words," Mel said. "I did confess I took someone else flea market hunting, but I don't think she holds it against you."

Court was having a hard time listening. She really did care what Mel was saying... but her fingers had developed a mind of their own and were traveling up over

Mel's knee, exploring the soft skin and gentle curves of her thighs.

Mel shifted beneath her, moving Court's hands a little higher, and when she spoke, her voice was huskier than before. "Do you want that tour now?"

Court shook her head. "I'm sure the apartment is great, but all I'm interested in now is right here in front of me."

She put one arm behind Mel's back, pulling her in for a kiss.

She breathed in her scent, Mel's bath products mixing with her natural aroma in a delicious way. She ran her tongue along Mel's lower lip, tasting and savoring her at the same time she teased her. And then she pressed into her mouth, desire exploding through her whole body as their tongues met.

Mel let out a low, satisfied moan, then took hold of Court's hand and guided it up higher, beneath her robe. Her legs parted and Court cupped her hand between Mel's thighs, feeling the soft, warm contours of her sex beneath her little cotton shorts.

God damn, Court wanted to rip them off her.

Mel's hips canted beneath her touch, and Court rubbed her fingers up and down, incredibly turned on as the thin fabric dampened. Mel moaned again, then kissed her way across Court's jaw.

"I've been wanting this for a while," Mel murmured, then closed her lips around Court's earlobe and breathed hot, tingly air into her ear.

She shivered, her own core instantly wet with desire. "Not longer than me, trust me."

Then she pushed the material of Mel's shorts aside and dipped one finger into the sweet, hot juices at her entrance. No underwear... Court had been pretty sure that was the case, but confirming it felt so good.

To Mel too, apparently, because she let out a plaintive cry against Court's ear then spread her thighs wider. "I want you. Now."

"What do you want?" Court teased, pressing one finger into her, only up to the second knuckle before pausing. "This?"

"Mmmore," Mel groaned, trying to move her hips against Court.

She could have kept teasing Mel, really drawn the whole thing out, but her own body was pulsing with need and this really had been a long time coming. She wasn't sure she had the willpower to make either of them wait any longer.

Court added a second finger, then thrust deeply inside, Mel's pussy clenching around her as her grip on Court's shoulder tightened.

"Oh my God," she breathed, rocking her hips. "That is so good."

Court smiled. "Good? I think I can do better than that..."

She shifted, laying Mel down on her back and dragging her drenched shorts off her in one quick motion. Mel's folds were glistening, her clit big and firm and begging to be licked. She spread her legs invitingly, but when Court started to crawl down to the other end of the couch so she could lay down between them, Mel caught her shirt in her hand and held her in place.

"I want to taste you too," she said, sitting up again and yanking Court's Fox County PD polo up over her head.

She quickly relieved her of her bra too, taking Court's large breasts into her hands and teasing one nipple with her tongue. It sent a lightning bolt of pleasure down her belly and between her legs, and Court scrambled to tear off Mel's robe and tank.

Her breasts were smaller, a perfect fit for the palms of Court's hands, her nipples pebbled and her warm skin the color of caramel.

Court's whole body was thrumming with desire moments later when she found herself lying beneath Mel, her head propped up on a pillow and her face buried between her thighs. Mel played her fingers up and down over Court's sex, circled her clit, plunged into her core in a dizzying sequence of sensations.

They were hungry for each other, starving after all this time looking but unable to touch. Now that the moment had finally come, Court wanted to devour this gorgeous woman.

Mel came first—Court made sure of that. Her thighs shook and her arms gave out on her, resting her full weight on Court as she completely lost herself to the moment. Court wrapped her arms around Mel's hips, holding her in place as she lapped ferociously at her clit and ran her tongue up and down through the slickness of her folds.

Court didn't last much longer after that. With Mel's thumb applying pressure to her clit and her fingers pumping in and out of her, Court felt her own orgasm building until she had no choice but to close her eyes and let it wash over her.

It was everything she'd been dreaming it would be ever since she finally met Mel in person... and she was far from sated.

As soon as her legs were no longer complete jelly, she nudged Mel off her and sat up, holding her hand out to her. "I'd like that tour now... be sure to show me the bedroom."

CHAPTER NINETEEN
MEL

*T*hey fell asleep in Mel's bed a while later, their limbs entangled and Court's head in the crook of Mel's arm. Mel was pleasantly exhausted, her body still thrumming with the aftershocks of her orgasms, and it was surprisingly easy to fall asleep with Court beside her.

How long had it been since she last shared her bed with someone, to actually sleep? Working the night shift wasn't exactly conducive to dating, and even when she did find someone she liked, they rarely had the same sleep schedule. Not that she'd had time for any of that lately, with Nonna's illness and working solo patrols.

Everything with Court came together so effortlessly though. She'd certainly taken the initiative when they first met, and it was hard to deny how much Mel wanted her when Court was so forward with her own desires.

Now, it was late afternoon and Mel was trying not to

CARA MALONE

move as she awoke, wanting to savor this moment as long as she could.

Court's chest softly rose and fell, just a thin sheet draped across her body. Mel was nestled into her, smelling the coconut of her hair and wondering what she was dreaming about. Court's eyelids fluttered slightly with REM sleep and, a minute later, they opened.

She let out a big yawn, her back arching as she stretched, then threw her arms around Mel and hugged her fiercely.

"Good morning," she said. "What time is it?"

"Definitely not morning," Mel said. She reached across Court to the side table where her phone was charging. No messages—that was a good thing these days. "It's four-thirty."

"Plenty of time before work," Court said, pouncing on her again as soon as Mel set down the phone. She kissed her, rolled onto her side and pressed one thigh in between Mel's legs.

"Mmm." Mel let out a groan, wrapping her arms around Court and grabbing her ass. "You feel so good."

How many times had they come this morning? And yet she was completely ready to dedicate the whole afternoon to more of the same.

"So do you," Court said into the crook of her neck, her warm breath making Mel shiver as it tickled her skin.

She grabbed the top edge of the sheet and pulled it up over her head, finding Court's breast with her mouth, then kissing and licking a trail further south.

"You're incredible, you know that?" Court said from

her side of the sheets once Mel was nestled between her thighs.

"So are you," Mel answered as she pushed into her and Court let out a pleased gasp.

*H*alf an hour later, Court was wearing Mel's bath robe and Mel had on a fresh pair of pajama shorts and a tank top as they made their way to the kitchen and she put on a pot of coffee.

"So, apart from the closet space, of which there's not much, I think this is the only room I haven't shown you yet," she said, putting her arms out and doing a little spin. "Voila. The grand tour is complete."

Court smiled, a wicked glint in her eyes, and she pushed Mel up against the counter. "I kinda feel like we should get it on in here... since we already did it in the living room and the bedroom."

"I can't say as I would object to that," Mel said, her hand going to the belt of her robe.

But then Court got distracted, looking over Mel's shoulder. "Oh my God, is that Custard Opal?"

Mel laughed as Court picked up the little Degenhart owl she'd spotted on the counter, its handwritten price tag still looped around its head. "You remembered the name."

"Did I get it right?" Court asked.

Mel turned the price tag over, showing her the identification. "Yup. I have a friend who works at one of the antique shops on the outskirts of town. She noticed this one at a vendor stall and called me."

Court whistled. "A hundred and fifty bucks... that's an expensive owl."

"A rare one," Mel said.

"Nonna's going to be psyched, right?" Court asked, and Mel grinned. Actually, she couldn't wait to show her grandmother her latest find, and if Court hadn't come over today, she would have already gone and presented it.

"The collection's one owl closer to completion." The percolator burbled out its last few drops and she reached into a cupboard for a couple of mugs.

"Does it count as a legitimate find if you have a friend keeping an eye out?" Court asked as Mel handed her a cup of steaming hot coffee.

"Yeah, I think so," she said. "It was still discovered out in the wild, so to speak," she said. "It's not like I bought it off eBay or anything."

"When are you going to show your grandma?"

"I was planning on going over there for dinner tonight, but—"

"I'm not keeping you, am I?" Court asked.

Mel pulled her into her arms and kissed her, enjoying the hint of hazelnut coffee and sweet cream on her lips. "Not at all... in fact, I'm not sure I'm ever gonna let you leave."

Court laughed. "Oh no, have I been kidnapped?"

"Maybe," Mel said cheekily. "Hey... crazy idea... do you want to come to dinner with me? You can meet Nonna."

Court's brows furrowed slightly and she studied Mel's face. "Are you sure you want me to? You and I have just started... whatever we're doing."

Mel picked up her mug, taking a sip and hiding behind it as she asked, "Dating?"

Court smiled wide. Damn, it was nice to be with someone who wore her heart on her sleeve and never left her questioning her status.

"Yes, dating," Court agreed.

"Well, then, it's totally natural for you to meet my grandma before—" Mel stopped abruptly. They both knew what she'd been about to say, but now that she'd caught herself, she couldn't even bring herself to complete the thought in her head.

Nonna was getting old. She was a fighter, but she was sick. And she would pass sooner or later—that was inevitable for everyone.

"I would love to meet Nonna," Court said, taking her hand and giving it a little squeeze. Then she looked down at herself in Mel's robe, the front of it beginning to gape open. "Although I should probably go home and change into something more dinner-appropriate... and let my dad know I narrowly escaped a kidnapping."

Mel laughed. "Please don't tell my boss I tried to kidnap you. It's not even true."

Court cocked an eyebrow at her. "You did threaten to, though."

"I don't know about that." Mel reached out and tugged on the belt, the robe spilling open. She set her mug down again and stepped inside the robe with

Court. If only every afternoon could be as sweet as this one...

---

*a*n hour and a half later, Mel was sitting in her car in the driveway of Nonna's house. She'd promised Court she wouldn't go inside without her, and she wondered if Nonna and Amanda had noticed her sitting in the driveway like a weirdo.

She didn't have to wait too long, though. Court pulled up to the curb in her mom's old car and stepped out wearing her dispatcher polo and khakis, a grocery bag looped over one arm.

"Hey," Mel greeted her at the sidewalk, leaning in to give her a kiss. "I told you not to bring anything."

Court held open the bag, revealing a juicy-looking mixed berry pie with a single slice cut out of it. "Well, I want to make a good impression... and when I got home I found this on the counter. I just know my dad was going to pig out on it once I left him to his own devices, so I cut him one slice and I'm saving him from himself by bringing the rest here." Mel chuckled, then Court asked, "Think anyone will mind there's a slice missing?"

Mel shook her head. "We're not stuck up around here when it comes to dessert. I'm just worried this is going to overshadow my Degenhart find."

They headed for the door and Court said, "Fat chance of that—I haven't met her yet but from everything

I've heard, your grandmother thinks the world of you. I'm sure my pie can't compete."

Inside, they found Amanda pulling takeout fried chicken out of containers and putting it on the dining table. Nonna was taking the lids off tubs of mashed potatoes, green beans and coleslaw, and Mel was relieved to see that she'd gotten some of her color back.

"Someone looks like she's feeling better," Mel said as she put her arm around Court and led her into the room.

"She's been talking my ear off about Kate and Toby all day," Amanda said, referring to Nonna's newfound obsession with *This is Us*.

"Toby is just perfect for her," Nonna said. "And Randall and Beth... that Susan Kelechi Watson is such a pretty lady."

"Well, Nonna, I'd like you to meet another pretty lady," Mel said. She led Court over to her. She'd called Nonna right after Court left her apartment to make sure it was okay to bring her, and Nonna had been excited to meet her. "This is Court Wilson. Court, my nonna, Gloria Pine."

"Oh, you can call me Nonna too, sweetie," she said, taking Court's hand in hers. "It's so nice to meet you."

"And she brought pie," Mel said.

"Ooh, it *sure* is nice to meet you," Amanda said with a wink.

Mel talked Amanda into staying long enough to eat, and then later, when she took off and it was just the three of them, they went into the living room to relax and talk a little while. Nonna was doing much better, and she'd been having breathing treatments at home so her lungs were clearer too.

She was pretty much equally thrilled about the mixed berry pie and the Degenhart owl, and she asked Court all kinds of questions about where she grew up and who her parents were and all the usual family-meeting-the-girlfriend topics. Court held her own, and by the time Nonna's night nurse arrived and it was time for Mel and Court to leave, Court was beaming.

"Your grandma is so sweet," she said as Mel walked her out to her car. "I'm glad I got to meet her."

"I'm sure she feels the same," Mel said. "And I do too."

"How was she when you first came out to her?" Court asked.

"Really good, actually," Mel said. "I was in high school, and nervous. My mom was long gone by then and I figured somebody of Nonna's generation... well, you know how that can go."

Court nodded.

"But she was always so supportive and accepting, no matter the subject," Mel said. Then she smiled. "And she's never admitted it, but I have a feeling from the way she's talked about some of her female friends when she was younger that if she'd grown up in different times, she might have dated a woman or two."

"It's never too late," Court said.

When they got to her car, Court leaned against the passenger door and Mel stepped close to kiss her. She tasted ever so faintly like blueberries, and Mel cursed the fact that she had to go to work tonight. It would have been nice to stay with Court.

"I wish you could have met my mom," Court said. "You would have loved her."

"I'm sure I would have."

"Well, Dad and I will have to have you over for dinner sometime," she said, brightening. "I mean, as soon as you're willing to admit to the chief that you're dating his daughter."

Mel laughed. "Is he the protective type?"

"Am I still a dispatcher and not a cop?" Court shot back.

Mel groaned. "Oh boy... will bringing pie help? Something low-sugar, because I don't want to be on your bad side, either."

Court wrapped her arms around Mel's shoulders, her wrists resting at the back of her neck. "The way to his heart is definitely his stomach... but I know he'll love you whether you bring dessert or not. I do."

Mel's eyebrows shot up and Court practically choked on her words.

"I mean... I like you a lot... it's kinda early to..."

"It's okay," Mel said, laughing again. "I know what you mean. And I... whatever... you too."

Court grinned. "Good. I'd hope so after what I did to you in your kitchen this afternoon."

CHAPTER TWENTY

*V*ee Mayfair was just walking out of her house, purse over one shoulder and lunch bag clutched beneath her elbow because she was trying to eat healthier, when she spotted a man and two women standing at the end of her driveway, near her car.

She startled, dropping her lunch bag on the stoop, and her heart started racing. Instantly, her thoughts went to thugs with weapons, people looking to rob her or just rough her up a bit. They were the thoughts of a woman who had spent years married to a heroin addict and knew the kind of violent people that lifestyle could attract.

Damn it... her mother always told her she should carry pepper spray on her keychain, but Eric's life wasn't her life anymore. She lived in a safe neighborhood now, where people didn't ordinarily loiter around her car.

She was just turning back toward the house, wondering if she could casually pretend to have forgotten something inside, when the man called, "Veronica Gilles?"

Oh God, he was coming closer...

"I'm Detective Tom Logan with the Fox County Police Department," he said, and all the blood drained out of her face.

Well, at least she knew he wasn't going to rob her in her own driveway to settle one of her husband's debts. Still... was it too late to pretend she hadn't heard him and duck back into the house?

No, that would look terrible, and she knew all about suspicious and dodgy behavior from Eric.

She turned and pasted on a smile. "It's Veronica Mayfair now. I took back my maiden name."

"Right, I'm sorry about that," the detective said. Then he gestured to the two women standing behind him. "These are my associates, Officer Mel Pine and Court Wilson. We just have a couple of questions about your husband, if you have a minute."

If I have a minute... Well, actually... Vee decided to try an evasion. She scooped her lunch bag off the concrete and said, "Actually, I need to get to work–"

"This will only take a minute," Detective Logan said.

Damn it.

Vee nodded, crossing her arms beneath her breasts in a show of impatience. "I'm not sure I can tell you much, I haven't spoken to Eric in a long time. What do you need from me?"

"Well, I'm told there was an altercation between you and Lydia Gilles at Eric's funeral last weekend," the detective said. His two *associates* stood slightly behind him like bodyguards, like they were ready to chase Vee down if she decided to run. One of them held a notebook and pen, poised to record what she said.

"Yeah, so?" Vee said. "Do you know anybody who gets along with their ex-mother-in-law?"

"I guess the argument was over her suggestion that you might stand to benefit financially from Eric's passing?" he said.

Vee watched cop shows. She knew all about this stuff, asking open-ended questions to get her talking, hoping she'd slip up and say something incriminating. She also knew she didn't have to talk to anybody about anything without a lawyer... as if she could afford that.

She shrugged, trying to get through this as quickly and painlessly as possible. "I might still be listed as his beneficiary," she said. "We're still legally married, although I'm sure that's something you've already looked up if you took the trouble to drive all the way out here."

"We did," the detective confirmed. "So, what was your relationship like with Eric, after you separated?"

Vee clenched her fist around her lunch bag, her arms wrapped around herself. "Non-existent, pretty much. There was no reason to keep in contact with him after I told him he could either seek help for his addiction or lose me. He chose the drugs."

"I'm sure that was upsetting."

She narrowed her eyes at the detective. "Upsetting enough to drive me to murder him for his death benefit? Is that what you're asking?"

He just stared right back at her, cool as a cucumber, and said, "You are not a suspect at this time. We just have questions."

"What else do you need to know?" Vee asked. She was getting short with him now and she was sure that wouldn't endear her to him, but she was going to be late clocking in and her boss was a stingy bastard who'd probably write her up for it. Not like she could say, *Well, the police were questioning me* by way of excuse.

Better just make this quick, then...

"Can you tell us a little about what your relationship was like when you were with him?" the detective asked. "Was he ever violent toward you, when he was on drugs or otherwise?"

The gears started turning in Vee's head. From hinting that she may have killed her ex for his pension to asking about domestic violence... Rachel had been in a wheelchair at the funeral, but Vee hadn't gotten to stick around long enough to ask what happened. Now she was wondering if Eric did that to her.

It wasn't like him though. She couldn't picture it.

"He never hurt me," she said. "All his demons were inside his own head."

Detective Logan just stood there, waiting for her to elaborate. Another crime show interrogation trick—make the suspect fill the uncomfortable silence.

This time, she was annoyed that it worked.

"He was a different person when he came back from Iraq," she said. "Sullen, introverted. I don't know what happened over there because he sure as hell never wanted to talk to me about it, but whatever it was, it fucked him up. He was injured and got put on prescription painkillers, but that's only part of why he ended up on street drugs. The rest of it was him trying to defeat, or maybe just mute, the mental demons he brought back from Iraq."

"Happens to the best soldiers," Logan said. "Did he ever seek treatment, therapy, drug rehabilitation?"

"Rehab, yes, but it never lasted," Vee said. "Therapy, no. His CO and his other Army buddies would never let him live it down if he admitted to needing that kind of help. Not *manly,* you know?"

She rolled her eyes.

"He was still in contact with his commanding officer?"

Vee nodded. "Guy lives a couple hours away. They'd talk online, see each other every once in a while."

"Were they close?"

"I wouldn't say so," Vee said. "Not like Eric and Adam. Those two were inseparable. I mean, hell, Adam married Eric's sister."

"Was there ever any resentment about that?" the detective asked. "Any animosity?"

Vee snorted. "No way. Eric looked at Adam like a brother. At some points in our marriage, Adam saw him more than I did."

She regretted it the minute that came out of her mouth. They'd been angling away from her and the windfall she stood to gain as long as that bitch, Lydia, didn't find a way to stop it, and now she'd just given these cops another reason to look at her sideways.

"Was that ever a point of contention between you and Eric?" the detective asked.

Damn it.

"No," she lied. "The only *point of contention* was Eric's drug use, and it sounds like that's what did him in at last. I wish I could say I'm surprised. But I'm just disappointed and sad for his family... and for him because he never managed to outrun his demons."

"Eric's mother mentioned that you may know who Eric bought drugs from," the detective pressed. Christ, how many more questions were there going to be? This was way more than a few.

"No, I don't know any of Eric's scumbag dealers," Vee snapped. "I hardly knew them back when we were together, and I sure as hell don't keep in touch with them now. Is there anything else, detective?"

She uncrossed her arms, putting her fists on her hips to illustrate her growing impatience. The detective looked backward at his two little cronies, and both of them shook their heads like they were denying the opportunity to cross-examine her.

"That'll be all today," he said, then pulled a business card out of his pocket and held it out to her. "In case you think of anything that may be relevant, here's my contact info. Thanks for talking to us."

"Mm-hmm," Vee said, snatching the card and stuffing it into her purse. She brushed past the three of them and got into her car, pulling out of the driveway before she'd even bothered to put on her seatbelt.

Goddamn Lydia, why'd she even have to give Vee's name to the cops in the first place? It wasn't like they'd spoken in the last five years, until Eric's death.

Vee was already ten minutes late and gritting her teeth with anger by the time she got to the end of the street. Instead of turning left to go to work, she went right to go through the Starbucks drive-thru. She sure as hell needed some sugar and caffeine to get through the rest of a day that started like this one, and if she was going to get written up anyway, what were a few more minutes?

*A*couple days after their excursion to talk to Veronica Mayfair, Court met up with Mel and Tom in the early evening to try to track down Eric's commanding officer.

Tom had a hunch that there was more to Eric's wartime trauma than just the injury to his knee and the terrible shit that anybody in active combat has to see and do. He wanted to talk to this CO that Eric had apparently kept in contact with, but he'd been a hard man to track down.

"Feels like the guy has been dodging my calls," Tom said when he'd called Court at home to tell her that he finally had an address for him. "Easy enough to get his name, Steven Larder, and a phone number, but his last known address is in New York and it's ten years old."

"And he won't answer the phone?" Court asked.

"Not so far," Tom grunted. "Though Veronica said that he and Eric mostly talked through email, so maybe that's just his MO. Anyway, I finally tracked down an address through his employer—I'm going to drop in on him tonight, hopefully get him right after work. Wanna come along?"

"I have work, but that's not til midnight," Court said. "I'll ask Mel, see if she wants to come too."

She did, of course. She and Court had been pretty much attached at the hip lately, except for when they had to work, and Court hadn't had to go far to ask Mel about visiting the CO. She'd been sitting on the couch right beside her, looking up the dates for various local garage sales, hoping to score that elusive Carnival Cobalt owl.

Now, it was about six o'clock, the sun beginning to set over the lake, and Mel and Court were driving to the address that Tom had given them. They were in Mel's car, which meant if they didn't have time to go back to her place and pick up Court's car after this meeting, they'd be carpooling to and from the precinct.

It was a small thing, but it made Court's belly go all warm and tingly every time she thought about it. *Carpooling to work with my girlfriend...* it had a nice ring to it, and it meant they'd be together in the morning when work ended. They could get breakfast together... maybe try the diner idea again... then go back to Mel's apartment and make love. God, she craved the feel of Mel's body against her own. And she liked falling asleep beside her almost as much.

She was beginning to fall in love... but it was still too soon to say those words.

Court reached across the center console and took

Mel's hand as she drove. "Do you think this guy's going to be able to tell us anything useful?"

"I don't know, the deployment to Iraq was twenty years ago," Mel said. She leaned forward, looking where Tom was leading them in the car ahead of them. "On the other hand... we seem to be pretty close to the place where Eric's body was burned."

"Seriously?"

Mel nodded. "We're probably only about five miles away. I noticed we were heading in that direction a while ago, and we just keep getting closer."

"That can't be a coincidence," Court said.

About ten minutes later, they came to a stop on the shoulder of the road behind Tom's unmarked police vehicle. It wasn't the same two-lane highway that Eric and his vehicle had been discovered on, but it was the same type of road—lots of trees on either side, pretty rural, with a few houses spaced far apart. They'd parked in front of a small ranch-style house that looked worse for the wear, and there was a pickup truck in the driveway.

"Looks like somebody's home," Mel said as she climbed out of the car. Court got out too and they met Tom at his rear bumper. Mel pointed out how close they were to the original crime scene.

"Yeah, I noticed too," Tom said. "Got kind of a bad feeling about that." Mel nodded, and Tom frowned at Court. "Maybe you better stay in the car, Wilson."

"No way. I came all the way out here."

"I'm not about to answer to your dad if something

happens to you," he argued back. "You're just shadowing —you don't have any actual training."

But Court stood her ground. "I'm not waiting in the car," she said, then started to walk toward the driveway before either of them could try to talk her out of it. "Come on."

Tom and Mel hurried to catch up to her, and by the time they got to the front door, they'd both stepped protectively in front of her. There was no doorbell, so Tom pulled open the screen to knock on the front door.

While they waited, Court looked around. The house was surrounded by woods, and she couldn't see lights from any of the surrounding homes through the thick foliage.

Tom knocked again, and somebody wrenched the door open from within. A man stood in front of them, large and imposing, with an irritated look on his face. "Help you?"

He sure didn't sound like he wanted to help anyone.

Court's attention was drawn to the high and tight crewcut, the bodybuilder shape of him.

"Hey," she said before she could stop herself, "You were arguing with Adam Tucker at Eric's funeral."

Tom's brows furrowed as he tried to play catchup, then suddenly the door was swinging shut. Acting on pure instinct, Tom stuck his foot in the door and said, "Fox County police, stop!"

The door rebounded off his foot, swinging open to reveal the man ducking into a room within the darkened house.

Tom put his hand on his gun, hooking his head to the side to motion Mel and Court back. Mel was reaching for her own gun, concealed in a holster beneath her jacket, and Court was realizing maybe she should have stayed in the car after all. Not only was she unarmed, Tom was right—she had no training for situations like this. She took a cautious step off the porch as Mel and Tom advanced.

"Mr. Larder?" Tom shouted into the house. Before he got any further, though, a piece of the doorframe exploded into splinters right beside his shoulder. There was a lightning crack and Court's hearing went tinny for a few seconds as she realized it had been a gunshot.

"Down!" Mel hissed, suddenly off the porch and at Court's side, pulling her into a crouch.

Court's heart was hammering in her chest and all she could think about was the fact that they were completely exposed in the front yard. If she wasn't killed here, her dad would probably finish the job once he found out she'd gotten herself into this situation.

"Shit," Mel muttered, bringing Court out of her thoughts.

She looked up to see Tom disappearing inside the house, gun drawn. Mel was fumbling her car keys out of her pocket.

"Go back to the car," she was saying, her words blurring together. "Lock yourself in and call 911—"

A burst of three or four shots erupted inside the house, so close to the front door that Court could actually

165

see the light from the muzzle flash. Then she heard something heavy drop.

"Oh God," Mel breathed, her gun up and pointed at the house.

"Tom," Court was saying, but Mel was dragging her to her feet, trying to push her toward the street.

"Go," she urged. "Stay low, move fast. I have to check on him."

Then she was gone, disappearing into the house. Court was glued in place a few feet away from Steven Larder's pickup truck, unable to move, barely able to think. All she could hear was her own blood rushing in her ears, and her dad's voice telling her leaving the dispatch office was too dangerous. An unacceptable risk.

And now, because she'd insisted on shadowing Tom through this case, because she'd dragged Mel along with her just to spend some time with a pretty girl, they were all in danger.

And here she was, frozen like a deer in headlights.

Useless.

Somewhere distant, she heard a door slam, and then the blood-chilling sound of footsteps rapidly getting closer. Steven Larder appeared around the side of the house, then stopped in his tracks when he saw Court standing next to his truck. Right next to the driver's side door.

Oh my God he's going to shoot me, I'm going to die right here, justlikemymother, justlike—

"Tom's been shot!"

Court snapped her head in the direction of Mel's

voice. She was running down the short flight of steps from the front door, telling Court they had to call it in, get an ambulance for him.

When Court looked back to the side of the house, Steven Larder was gone.

"Court!" Mel was demanding her attention and it felt like all the joints in her neck had turned to molasses as she dragged her head back to look at her. "Did you call the police?"

Mel was at her side now, pulling her up against the side of the truck for cover.

"No," Court said. Was this what shock felt like? Didn't you actually have to be *involved* in an incident to go into shock? All she'd done was stand there.

Mel pulled her phone out and started to dial. She was clumsy at it because she had Tom's handgun as well as her own now, and she was going to have to do everything because Court was shutting down. She was definitely not ready for the police academy.

Vaguely, Court was aware of Mel's side of the conversation. She said, "officer down," and gave dispatch the address, telling them what happened to Tom.

And then Court caught some motion from the corner of her eye. She snapped her head to the left, where she heard the sound of leaves crunching underfoot and twigs snapping as someone ran through the woods, away from the house.

"Mel!" she said, pointing. "There he goes!"

She'd come out of that momentary fogginess and now everything was crystal clear. This guy had been hard for

Tom to track down, like he was trying not to leave a foot-print, and now he was disappearing again. He'd shot Tom —Court didn't even know if he was still alive—and the man had obviously had something to do with Eric's death or he wouldn't have gone for his gun the minute he heard the word 'police.'

"We have to go after him!" she said.

"Fuck no," Mel said. "We're waiting for backup, and Tom needs an ambulance." Then she was talking to the dispatcher on the phone again. "I used my belt to put on a tourniquet, but he's still inside the house... Yeah, upper thigh."

Shit, that was bad. If the femoral artery had been nicked, a tourniquet wouldn't do much good, even if an ambulance was nearby. And way out here... fat chance of that.

Tom could die, and Larder was about to disappear into those woods.

"We can't let him get away," Court said, pleading with Mel even though she was too distracted to listen.

"...yes, I think it's safe to go back into the house," she was telling the dispatcher. "The suspect has fled..."

"I'm going after him," Court said.

The decision came out of the blue—certainly not out of the logical, self-preserving part of her brain. She was thinking about her mother and how the fact that her killer was behind bars was a small comfort to Court and her dad. She was thinking that Steven Larder didn't deserve to run away from this and never face justice for what he did to Tom, what he likely did to Eric Gilles.

And then, before she could think better of it, she grabbed Tom's gun out of Mel's hand, and then she ran.

Toward the woods, toward the rustle of leaves and snap of twigs, toward a man who had a secret he was desperate to keep.

"Court!" she heard Mel shout behind her. "Courtney, get back here!"

She'd never heard her full name on Mel's lips before. She rarely heard it at all these days, except from her dad. She was always either Court or Wilson or the chief's daughter or dispatch.

But to her parents, to her mom especially, she was always Courtney.

I love you, Courtney, baby. Did you finish your homework, Courtney? Courtney Marie, don't you give me that look! Have a good day and be safe, Courtney-girl.

It only made her run harder.

CHAPTER TWENTY-TWO
MEL

"Court, no!"

Mel was shouting at the top of her lungs, but Court disappeared into the woods.

"Fuck," she grunted, her mind racing with the different paths she could take. Go back inside the house and try to keep Tom from bleeding out in spite of the tourniquet. Run to the road and wait for the ambulance to arrive, make sure they didn't miss the house on this dark, rural road.

Or, what her heart was telling her to do, go after Court. Keep her safe from this lunatic who just shot Tom and probably killed Eric Gilles too.

Oh God.

There was really only one valid choice to be made. Tom wasn't mortally wounded—he was still conscious, although probably not too happy about it. He could keep pressure on his own wound until the medics arrived. Court, on the other hand, had just gone running into the woods after a killer, holding a gun she didn't know how to shoot.

"Fuck, fuck, fuck..." Mel muttered as she ran back into the house. She found Tom where she'd left him on the floor of the dingy living room, both hands wrapped around his thigh and his back pressed up against an ancient plaid sofa. She crouched beside him. "Court's gone."

"What?"

"She ran after the perp," she said. "I'm going after them both."

"Go," Tom told her without hesitation.

"You got your phone on you?" Mel asked. He nodded, sucking air through his teeth as he tried to shift his leg, tried to find a comfortable position. Mel put her hand on his shin. "Don't move. I called 911—an ambulance will be here soon."

"Soon-ish," Tom corrected. They were pretty far from downtown and he knew it.

"You'll be okay," Mel said. "Tell them we went on foot into the woods behind the house, heading northwest, I think."

That was all she had time for. She couldn't let Court and Steven Larder get so far away she wouldn't be able to track them, and it was likely to be pitch-black in those woods. If it was anybody but Court, Mel would wait for backup. She wouldn't be stupid enough to go running after them with nothing but her service revolver.

All of that was racing through her head, and then Tom squeezed her arm, pulling her out of her thoughts.

"Go," he said. "She needs you."

Mel nodded and got to her feet. She took one deep, centering breath, then ran back out the front door and cut through the yard and into the woods. While she ran, trying unsuccessfully to avoid sticks and leaves that would crunch underfoot and give her away, all those worried thoughts and diverging choices disappeared.

Her mind went radio-silent and all her senses sharpened.

Her eyes adjusted to the dark. Her ears pricked at every little sound from the forest. Her hand gripped the butt of her gun, and even in the dark, she sensed that she was following a path. Steven Larder was leading her and Court somewhere he'd gone before.

Mel knew from all her years on the force that it would be somewhere wrought with danger and she just hoped she caught up to Court before she caught up to Larder.

CHAPTER TWENTY-THREE

*T*he bitch was following him.

He'd been running for at least a mile and he could still hear her back there—crunching on leaves and huffing and puffing like she'd never tailed anybody before in her life, but keeping up nonetheless.

When he'd come around the side of the house, wanting to get in his truck and floor it the fuck out of there, she just stood there and stared at him, like an enemy combatant who just realized he done fucked up and found himself in the sights of Steven's rifle. She was damn lucky the second female cop had come out of the house right in that moment, otherwise she would have ended up just like all the Iraqis he'd left dead in his wake.

It was either take the time to raise his gun and shoot her like he shot the cop who'd had the balls to let himself into the house, or make a clean getaway.

Well, that's what he'd thought he was doing, anyway.

Who would have guessed she'd be crazy enough to run after him?

He thought about popping off a couple warning shots, scaring her off, but who knew what other surprises this chick had up her sleeve? He'd learned his lesson about ammo conservation when he was on active duty and he wasn't about to get himself killed by some lady cop out in the woods, on his own damn property, just because he ran out of bullets.

No, sir.

So he kept running, hoping like hell he'd lose her before he got to the cabin. He needed some time when he got there to gather up the goods and his bug-out bag. If he didn't lose her, he'd have to kill her and he wasn't a *complete* idiot. He wasn't about to kill a cop.

He'd shot the trespassing one, but that was just a flesh wound. After twenty years in the military, Steven knew the difference between a glancing blow and a kill shot, and he also knew the punishment for murdering cops. All the stolen Iraqi gold in the world wasn't worth that, even if he *had* waited twenty years for this moment.

He just kept running, wondering if he should change course, forget the cabin. Could he come up with some kind of diversion to throw this chick off? All that huffing and puffing, she was obviously not used to pursing suspects on foot, and yet some Terminator-like drive just kept her pounding after him.

Fucking Eric, he found himself thinking, clenching his jaw as he picked up his pace.

He always had been the weak link in this plan. If it

had been up to Steven, he never would have looped him in. But Gilles was Tucker's best friend and Tucker said he wouldn't play along unless they cut Gilles into the deal.

Shoulda followed my gut, Steven thought. *Shoulda figured out a way to keep all the fucking gold for myself, forget both of those assholes.*

He spotted his destination up ahead, an ancient hunting cabin not much bigger than a shed, barely visible in the dark. If you didn't know it was there, you'd never see it through the thick undergrowth of the forest. That gave him an idea.

He made an abrupt left turn, away from the cabin. He ran until he was sure the Terminator chick behind him had made the turn too, and then he cut back in the direction of the cabin as silently as possible.

All he needed was five minutes. Five minutes to gather what he needed, and then he'd be gone, like he was never fucking here at all.

CHAPTER TWENTY-FOUR
COURT

*T*he little cabin in the forest had rotting wooden siding and the shingles on the roof looked like they'd had better days... many, many years ago. It looked like nobody had bothered with so much as locking the door, let alone any sort of real upkeep, in a long time, and Court inched up to it as quietly as she could. There was no way it was even a little bit soundproof, and she knew Larder was inside.

She'd followed him on a winding path through the woods, managing to keep track of him against all odds. She'd even lost him at one point, but the heavy ground-cover of last year's fallen leaves helped her pick up his trail again as he crunched through them. Was it luck, or was he really luring her to a remote location so he could shoot her and then burn her body like he'd done to Eric Gilles?

The deeper into the woods she got, the more certain

she was that Steven Larder had been the arsonist. If he wasn't, why had he run?

And if he was, why the hell was she still chasing him?

This had to be in the top five dumbest things she'd ever done—maybe even number one with a bullet—and when her dad found out, they should have an ambulance on hand because he'd probably have a coronary. He sure wasn't going to let her take the civil service exam now.

But her body had reacted before her brain had a chance to tell her what a colossally dangerous thing she was doing. Once she was running through the woods, it seemed like the only way out was to catch up to Larder and detain him.

Now, crouching low outside the shack, her back to the wall and Tom's handgun clutched in both of her hands—pointing at the ground like she'd seen on TV cop shows—it was time to prove her mettle. Put up or shut up, and all that cliché crap.

She could hear Larder inside, along with the damp, dull sound of rotting wood being ripped up and tossed aside. He was armed and definitely better-trained than she was. He was also bigger and stronger than her, and he had a hell of a lot less to lose. That meant she had only one chance to take him by surprise and get the upper hand.

If she messed up, he'd shoot her without hesitation and that'd be the end for her.

Looking down at the gun in her hands, she could just make out the safety switch in the low light. *Safety off... I hope,* she thought. Staying low, she inched her way around to the cabin door, which Larder had left open, probably so he could make a speedy escape. So much the better for Court—no creaky doors to open, no advance warning.

Three, two, one...

She jumped into the open doorway, pistol raised, and shouted at the top of her lungs, "Freeze, motherfucker!"

Okay, so maybe she'd seen a few too many cop shows. Still, it had the desired effect. Caught off guard, Larder froze in place for a split second, allowing her to take in the scene. He'd ripped up a couple of floorboards and had a grungy Army-issue rucksack open at his feet, something metallic and shimmering inside of it.

His momentary freeze didn't last long. In the blink of an eye, he was reaching for the gun beside the rucksack and Court had to make a decision. She pointed her gun at the floor near him and squeezed the trigger.

The rotten wood exploded in a million splinters at Larder's feet and his gun fell through the old floorboards.

Thank God for that, Court thought. She had no illusions about how lucky she'd just gotten. That could have gone a lot of different ways, most of them ending with her being shot. But now she had a gun, and Larder didn't. She raised the muzzle, pointing it at him.

"I said freeze," she barked, trying to make her voice as hard and authoritative as possible. "Stand up straight. Keep your hands where I can see them."

She was running on instinct now, and a half-dozen memorized lines from TV. As she talked, she scanned the room to be sure that there were no other weapons lying around, and as her eyes adjusted to the light inside the cabin, she realized that the glimmering goods inside the rucksack were a tangle of small gold bars and jewelry.

So not what she'd been expecting. Drugs, sure, but gold hidden beneath the floorboards in an old hunting cabin in the woods? What the hell was going on here?

"Listen, I'm not going to jail," Larder said, one of his hands drifting downward. "What if we–"

He seemed to be reaching for the rucksack. Trying to bribe her, maybe? This was a hell of a time to realize that she had no handcuffs, no radio, nothing but the gun in her hands to help her control this guy... and with the way she'd taken off running into the woods, who knew if Mel could trace them to this cabin?

For the first time, Court realized that she could well be in a standoff that only ended when either she or Steven died. She had a gun, but he was a trained soldier.

Fuck.

"Shut up!" she barked. "Put your hands back up!"

He put his hands up, but he didn't stop talking. "This jewelry, the gold... all of it is totally off the books. Nobody knows it's here except you and me... and Eric, but you already know what happened to him."

His hand was drifting downward again, slowly, like he thought she might not notice if he kept her distracted. "Stop moving!"

"I'll split it with you," he pressed on. "First it was gonna be three ways—me, Adam, Eric—but now we're down to two. And Adam owes me a favor for disposing of the body, so now I'm thinking you and I—"

"I'm serious!" Court barked, but even she could hear her voice wavering. This guy just would not stop reaching for that rucksack. "Freeze or I shoot!"

He smiled. "You don't have the balls, or you would have done it already."

Then he moved, one fast blur of activity, swooping down and picking something up off the floor as he dodged to the left of where Court's gun was aimed. But what he grabbed wasn't jewelry. Court had just a second to notice the glint of cold metal in the moonlight as Larder came at her with a three-inch blade that must have been in the rucksack.

She closed her eyes, squeezed the trigger again, and screamed when she felt a hand closing around her wrist.

Blood rushed into her face. There was the deafening ring of the gunshot. Court waited to feel the icy pain of the blade penetrating her flesh.

And then Mel's voice was in her ear, saying, "Court, are you okay? Courtney!"

She opened her eyes. Mel wrapped her arm across Court's chest as she pulled her out of the doorway, her service pistol hovering over Court's shoulder, pointing at Larder.

Larder was slumped against the wall, one hand pressed to his stomach, blood seeping through his shirt and pooling in his lap.

Court's mind raced to catch up with all of that, and Mel spun her around just outside the door, pressing her up against the cabin as if she was worried she might collapse.

"Are you okay?" she asked again. "He didn't hurt you, did he?"

All Court could do was shake her head. And then Mel was gone, disappearing through the door of the cabin.

"Don't move!" she growled at Larder. Court heard the skittering sound of the blade being kicked away, and then the distinctive metallic click of handcuffs being slapped into place. Then Mel called for her. "Court, can you help?"

She snapped out of her stupor. "Yes," she called, going back into the cabin. "What do you need me to do?"

"He's cuffed, he can't hurt you," Mel said. "Can you put pressure on the wound? Or would you rather call—"

"I'll do it," Court said before Mel could finish giving her an alternative.

She crouched down on the floor next to Larder, who was laid out flat now and giving her a death glare, but he was gut-shot and handcuffed, and he posed no threat to her. Now she just wanted to make sure he didn't bleed out before he paid for his crimes.

She put both hands on his stomach, grimacing slightly at the warmth of the blood pooling on his abdomen. He grimaced too as she pressed down to staunch the flow, and she told Mel, "He confessed to disposing of Eric's body. They stole all of that—during the war, I guess."

She nodded to the gold and jewelry spilling out of the rucksack.

"Don't worry," Mel said. "Tom's a good detective—he

won't stop until he's uncovered every single illegal thing this asshole has done and prosecuted him for it."

"He's okay?" Court asked.

Mel nodded. "The paramedics are with him right now. He's going to make a full recovery." She got out her phone, calling dispatch to give them directions to the cabin.

It wasn't long before Court could hear voices in the woods, coming closer. While they were alone—well, alone except for Larder, who was quickly losing consciousness from the blood loss—she said, "Thanks, Mel. For saving me."

Mel kissed her. "You don't need anybody to save you... but I'll always have your back."

Then Mel stood, and suddenly the tiny cabin was filled with more people than Court would have thought possible. Somebody took over putting pressure on the wound, and Mel pulled Court to her feet.

"Come on," she said. "Let's get out of here."

CHAPTER TWENTY-FIVE

*A*dam Tucker sat in a tiny, cinderblock-walled interrogation room at the precinct. He'd been there for at least two hours already without a single person so much as poking their head in to tell him how much longer he was going to have to wait.

He'd never been interrogated before, but he knew this was all part of the game. Make him uncomfortable. Keep him guessing.

And he sure as hell was guessing.

It had been a little after midnight when the police had come and pounded on his door. He'd just said goodnight to Rachel, who was still sleeping in the guest bedroom downstairs, and gone up to the master bedroom to take a shower and climb into their big marital bed all by himself for another night.

When she first came home from the hospital, she said it was because she was weak. She was still relying on the wheelchair a fair amount and didn't want to try to deal

183

with the stairs. Adam knew she was pissed, though, and after a couple days of sleeping apart, Rachel stopped pretending it was because of her injury.

He wasn't sure their marriage was going to survive all this, even though he'd done everything for her in the first place. That's what he'd been thinking about when he heard an angry fist practically beating down the front door.

He'd ended up getting arrested in his bathrobe, with nothing but his boxers underneath, and the dirtbag cops that had come for him couldn't even give him—a veteran, for fuck's sake—the courtesy of letting him put real clothes on.

"Adam Tucker, you're under arrest for trafficking stolen merchandise," the officer had said as he slapped the cuffs on him. Rachel just scowled at Adam when she heard that. But then the officer added, "And the murder of Eric Gilles."

And that's when she'd screamed and slumped onto the couch. The last glimpse of his wife that Adam got was with her face buried in her hands, sobbing as the cops hauled him outside. They had the blue and red lights flashing on the squad car and everything, just to make sure all the neighbors came out to watch his humiliation.

Now, after two hours with nothing to do but think about his situation, Adam was feeling pretty angry. He just couldn't decide who to be mad at.

Rachel, for not seeing what he'd sacrificed for her, so she could live the lifestyle she wanted with a big house and a nice car and a freakin' purebred Samoyed.

Eric, for walking in on him and Steven at the worst possible moment twenty damn years ago—just as they were packing up the stolen goods—and proceeding to have a moral crisis that lasted two decades.

Or maybe Steven, who clearly didn't know what 'take care of it' meant and who'd gotten Adam into this huge fuckin' mess in the first place. And who was God knew where right now, probably disappearing like he always did when it suited him. It should have been him in this interrogation room, not Adam.

What he did know was that the cops couldn't possibly have anything on him besides suspicion. Adam's hands were clean. He'd made damn sure of that.

The door handle rattled slightly, and the door swung open at last. Adam sat up straight, trying not to look as impatient and irritated as he felt, and crossed his arms over his chest. "About goddamn time."

The two chick cops who'd been at the hospital with that detective walked into the room, along with a third officer who Adam didn't recognize. The new one carried an Army-camouflaged rucksack and slammed it heavily down on the stainless steel table in front of Adam. Then he stepped back, arms crossed, eyes narrowed at Adam.

Ignoring the bag, Adam asked one of the women, "Where's your buddy? Hogan, was it?"

"Logan," the blonde one said.

"Never mind him," the other woman, the one with *Officer Pine* embossed on a little gold nameplate on her breast pocket, said. She unzipped the rucksack, pulling it open in front of Adam. "Why don't you tell us about this?"

He leaned forward, made a show of inspecting the contents of the bag as if it was the first time he'd ever seen it. In fact, it'd been twenty years since he'd last seen it all in one place, and he was glad he wasn't hooked up to any kind of biometric readers because his heart beat sped up at the sight of it.

There was about a million dollars' worth of Iraqi gold bars and assorted jewelry in that rucksack, or at least that's what Steven had told him when they were squirreling it away all those years ago. *We just have to play the waiting game, hold onto it for a while until it's safe to start selling it off. It'll be worth the wait,* he'd promised.

Yeah, so much for that plan.

Adam shrugged, looked at Officer Pine. "What, you bring your jewelry box into work tonight? Those chains're gonna take a while to unknot—you should really store 'em better than that."

"We know this was illegally transported out of Iraq," Mel said. "Your commanding officer, Steven Larder, admitted as much to us."

"Well, it sounds like Sergeant Larder is going to need a lawyer, then," Adam said. "But why does Fox County PD care about that? Sounds like a problem for the military courts."

"You're right about that, and we'll be notifying a local court martial first thing in the morning," Pine said. "What we're concerned with is Eric Gilles' death, and the desecration of his corpse."

Adam was starting to get downright pissed. They'd had him in this room for two hours in the middle of the damn night, they arrested him in front of his whole neighborhood and made his wife hate him even more than she already did, and this was the best they had?

"I had nothing to do with that," he said. "Eric was my brother-in-law and my brother in arms. I would never hurt him, and I couldn't burn his body. Besides, you know I was at the hospital with Rachel that night."

"But you're probably not too broken up about the fact that he's not around causing problems for you anymore," the blonde one suggested. Then she reached into the back pocket of her pants.

Adam's heart skipped a beat as he looked at what she was laying on the table in front of him. He summoned every ounce of Army training he'd ever received to keep his face neutral as he looked at the necklace she'd produced.

Delicate gold chain. Heart-shaped emerald pendant with a ring of diamonds around it—Rachel had called it a green Heart of the Ocean, after that nineties chick flick movie with what's his pretty-boy face, DiCaprio. It was the prettiest thing they'd brought home from Iraq, and Adam had asked Steven for it when Larder at last announced that it would be safe to start selling off their loot.

"What's that?" Adam asked.

"The necklace you gave your wife on your last anniversary," the blonde said. "The one her brother saw around her neck the afternoon that he died, that made him freak out and fight with her because he knew what you and Steven were doing was wrong."

Adam couldn't help it. His jaw went a little bit slack at that and he knew his guilt was written all over his face. Guilt in addition to shock, because the only way they could know all that—the only way they could have that necklace—was if Rachel gave it to them.

"Thought that might jog your memory," the blonde said, then stepped back so Officer Pine could have another go at him.

"Rachel told us everything," she said. "She just finished giving her statement."

Ah, so that's what the two-hour wait was all about. They needed to buy time while his wife sold him up the river. Great.

Anger boiled in Adam's veins and it was a Herculean effort to keep a straight face as he stared back at Pine, steeled his jaw and asked, "So? What do you need me for then?"

"We know that it was Steven Larder's idea to steal all this from the Iraqi citizens you were sent there to protect—"

"We were sent there to keep them from looting their own cities," Adam objected, but Pine held up a hand.

"Save it for the military court system," she said, then went on. "We know Rachel and Eric got in a fight when he recognized the necklace you gave her, and that he'd been feeling guilty for being involved in the whole scheme. And we know Steven's the one who burned Eric's body. But I'm thinking you're the one who walked in on Eric and Rachel fighting. I think he shoved Rachel into the counter and you got so angry you killed him, then told Steven to dispose of the body."

Adam clenched his fists, then slowly unfurled them. "What did Rachel say about it?"

"I'm asking you," Pine answered.

"I didn't kill him," Adam said. "You're right—he is the reason Rachel ended up in the hospital. But it was an accident. He tried to snatch the necklace right off her neck and she tripped over the dog trying to get away from him. But he was alive the last time I saw him. I didn't lay a finger on him—I just told Steven to get him out of my sight."

"So you orchestrated a hit," Pine suggested.

"No!" Adam pounded both fists on the table, making the jewelry dance in front of him. "Whatever he did to Eric after they left my house was Steven's call. I didn't say to kill him—he was my best friend. Now I want a damn lawyer!"

Officer Pine just smirked at him, like she hadn't heard a damn word he'd said, then turned to the other two cops and said, "Let's go."

She and the blonde walked out, and the third, silent cop came over and snatched all the jewelry and the ruck-sack off the table, then let the door slam hard on the way out. Adam just sat there, staring at the table, wondering what the hell he'd lost his best friend for, and was prob-ably going to lose his wife for.

Nothing.

CHAPTER TWENTY-SIX
MEL

*A*fter they got done interviewing Adam Tucker, Mel and Court went to the hospital to check on Tom in the early morning.

In the car on the ride over, Mel sat in the passenger seat, her body still humming with the adrenaline of everything that had happened. It would drain out of her soon, and then she'd probably crash. But for now, she squeezed Court's hand and felt wide-awake and energized.

"I can't believe you chased after Larder like that," she was saying as Court pulled into the hospital parking garage.

"I know... it was reckless, but I couldn't let him get away," she answered.

"I shouldn't be encouraging you," Mel said, nibbling her lower lip and trying to hold the words back before she blurted, "but it was kinda sexy watching you train that gun on him and bark orders."

"Oh yeah?" Court's eyes were glittering with something a little wild when she pulled into a parking space and turned to look at her. She probably had even more adrenaline coursing through her system than Mel, who desperately wanted to climb across the gearshift and straddle her.

She let go of Court's hand so she could tuck a tendril of golden hair behind her ear. "Don't ever do it again without proper police training, though. I don't think I could bear to lose you."

Court nodded. "I promise."

Then she leaned closer, cupping Mel's face in both her palms, pulling her in until she could plant a long, deep kiss on her lips.

When at last they came out of it, Court let out a nervous chuckle and said, "God, I can't imagine what my dad's gonna say. I might need to flee the state."

Chief Wilson knew everything that had happened in the last few hours. He was the one who had allowed Mel and Court to question Adam Tucker since Tom was out of commission. But the chief was holed up in his office, swamped with press inquiries and requests from the military court martial. Court had been artfully avoiding him so far.

"Will you come with me?" she asked.

Mel grinned. "I'd follow you anywhere." They kissed again, then she added reluctantly, "Right now, though, we should probably go check on Tom."

They went into the hospital, their hands linked as they navigated the labyrinthine halls until at last they found a uniformed policeman standing guard outside a private room in the emergency department.

"Logan in there?" Mel asked. She recognized the guard—name was O'Connell, and he was a night shift guy like Mel.

In fact, she was supposed to be patrolling right now too—it was about five a.m.—but she and Court were both on administrative leave for the next few days. They'd have to talk to the precinct psychologist about the shoot-out, and Court would have to answer to the fact that she'd basically gone vigilante when Larder took off running into the woods.

But her dad was the chief. Mel was sure everything would turn out okay.

"Hey, Pine," O'Connell said, nodding at her. "Yeah, he's sleeping. They gave him something for the pain."

"Sedated?" she asked.

He shook his head. "Just painkillers."

"Mind if we go in?" She was still holding Court's hand, and truth be told, she never wanted to let her go again.

"Visiting hours are over," O'Connell pointed out. "I'll fend off the nurse for you."

"Thanks," she said, then led Court into the room.

The overhead lights were off, with just a task light in one corner keeping the room dimly lit. Tom had the room to himself, and Mel knew that he was a bachelor and his parents had both passed. There would be coworkers from the precinct visiting later in the day, and she was pretty sure Tom had a brother somewhere who'd probably want to come. But he didn't have anybody at his bedside right now, nobody worrying over him and keeping watch except for O'Connell in the hallway.

Up until a few weeks ago, this is exactly what it would have looked like if Mel found herself in a hospital bed in the middle of the night. Nonna would want to come, of course, and so would Zara and Kelsey... but would any of them actually show up and keep vigil through the night?

Now she had Court, though, and she knew without a doubt that the nurses would need the Jaws of Life to pry Court away from her if she was in the hospital. It was a nice feeling, even though she hoped it'd never actually happen.

Tom's eyelids fluttered as he became aware that he wasn't alone in the room.

"Hey, buddy," Court said, pulling Mel closer to the bed. "You awake?"

Tom grunted and his eyes opened, narrow slits that were struggling against the meds and the pain. "Larder didn't shoot you, huh?"

"Good to see you too," Court huffed.

Mel pulled a couple stiff hospital chairs next to the bed, and Tom reached for the button to raise himself into a sitting position. Mel poured him some water from a plastic pitcher, moving on instinct because it was exactly what she would have done for her nonna. She held the cup while he drank greedily from a straw, then let his head plop back on the pillow.

CARA MALONE

"Thanks," he said. "These painkillers give me incredible cottonmouth."

"How are you feeling?" she asked.

"Like I got shot," he said. "But I'll live. What about Larder?"

"They tell us he'll live too," Court said. "He came after me with a knife and Mel shot him."

"Serves him right," Tom said, holding out a fist to Mel.

They bumped, and he gestured for a little more water while Mel and Court caught him up on everything he missed—the jewelry and gold Larder had hidden under the floorboards of his cabin, how fast he'd been to rat out Tucker, and how it hadn't taken much to make Tucker's own wife turn on him as well.

"So who actually killed Gilles?" Tom asked, squinting as he tried to process everything. "Tucker?"

"He's pointing the finger at Larder," Mel said, "who is currently in surgery. As soon as he's able to be questioned, we'll get to the bottom of it."

"Pine and Wilson are on the case," Tom said, a goofy, drugged-up grin on his face.

Court patted his arm. "We'll let you get some rest. We just wanted to check on you and let you know what was going on."

"'Preciate it," he said. "Thanks for not letting me die out there."

"Anytime," Mel answered.

They said their goodbyes and Mel gave O'Connell a nod on their way out. Court looped her arm into Mel's as

194

they meandered their way back toward the parking lot. Court checked her phone and said she'd gotten a couple of texts from her dad.

"He'll be busy for a while," she said. "It's five-thirty in the morning and the rest of the day is ours. What should we do with it?"

"Well, I've got one idea," Mel said, pleased when she noticed that there was still a little bit of adrenaline in her system, a little more energy that needed burning off.

Court raised an eyebrow. "Oh yeah?"

"Let's go back to my place," she suggested. "I want to check you over from head to toe, you know, just to make sure you're really okay."

"That's a good idea," Court agreed. "Safety first... and my thighs are awfully sore after all that running."

"Don't worry, I'll get you off your feet," Mel said. "And I'll give you a nice massage, paying special attention to your thighs and all the surrounding areas until you're feeling tip-top again."

"You're too good to me," Court said, and Mel wrapped her arm around Court's shoulder, pulling her close so she could kiss her temple while they walked.

"Not true," she said. "You deserve all the goodness in the world."

"You're all I need," Court responded, her hand sliding down to squeeze Mel's ass and give it a playful swat.

*T*hey went back to Mel's apartment, and this time there was no pretense of a tour. Court went straight for the bedroom the moment they were in the door, losing layers as she went. Mel hurried after her, and found Court lying stretched out on the bed.

"Come here, baby," she said, hooking a finger at her.

She was down to her bra and panties, a silky set that nearly matched her skin tone. Mel could see the outlines of her pert nipples and a growing dampness between her thighs, and it was just about the best sight she'd ever laid eyes on.

"God, you're beautiful," she said. She traced every one of Court's delicious curves with her eyes, slowly drinking her in while she undid the buttons on her uniform shirt.

"I need you," Court murmured, batting her lashes and doing her damnedest to drive Mel crazy. It was working.

She shimmied out of her trousers and crawled into bed in nothing but a sports bra and a pair of boy shorts. Mel straddled one of Court's thighs, enjoying the view as she looked down at her on her back, and when Court reached up to touch her, Mel swatted her hand away.

"I told you, I want to take care of you," she said. She leaned forward, bracing herself on either side of Court's shoulders, their eyes locking from just a few inches apart. "I want to lavish attention on you and make you feel good."

"Mmm..." Court bit her lip, squirming beneath her,

obviously struggling not to touch her. "Just don't take too long."

Mel brought her knee up higher, her thigh pressing against Court's panties. She could feel her wetness, even through the fabric. "Are you hot for me?"

Court nodded emphatically. "So hot."

Mel lay down beside her and lifted one of Court's hands. She brought her fingertips to her mouth, kissing the pad of each finger before bringing Court's hand down and sliding it beneath her shorts. "Me too."

"Oh God," Court groaned, her fingers sliding up and down over Mel's pussy. She brushed her clit and an electric jolt sent a shiver up Mel's spine. Her eyes fluttered shut and she knew if she didn't stop now, she'd lose all her willpower.

She pulled Court's hand away, kissing her fingers again and tasting herself on her girlfriend. That's what Court was, right? Her girlfriend, her partner?

Maybe forever?

Mel looked deep into those big blue eyes, searching for Court's feelings on the subject. She didn't need to look far—Court's emotions were always written all over her face, and right now she looked like pure bliss.

Mel got back on her knees, crawling down to the foot of the bed and dragging Court's panties down her legs as she went. Court arched her back, unclasped her bra. She threw it aside and flopped back on the pillow as Mel teased her exposed sex with one finger. She circled around her clit, enjoying the way Court melted into the bed and the way the scent of her arousal made Mel light-headed in the best of ways.

She moved her hand lower, pressing into her core as she brought her mouth down to taste and savor and lavish her.

"You taste so good," she groaned as Court threaded her fingers into Mel's hair, pulling her ponytail loose.

"You feel amazing," Court murmured back.

"We haven't even gotten to the foot massage yet," Mel pointed out, and Court pushed her head back down.

"We're past that, babe."

Mel buried her face in Court's sex, working enthusiastically until she felt Court's thighs clench around her head. Best feeling in the world. Court shuddered and moaned, and Mel felt the contractions of her body against her hand, the flood of juices on her tongue. Making Court come was fast becoming one of her favorite things —even better than getting off herself—and she lingered between her thighs until every last quiver had subsided.

Then she crawled up to the top of the bed, wiping her chin on the corner of the bedsheet and then pulling Court into her arms. "You're the best thing that's ever happened to me."

Court grinned, lifting her head and looking Mel in the eyes. It would have been so much easier to confess her feelings if she could do it while staring at the ceiling, but Court just wasn't that kind of girl. She was grinning straight at her.

"Really?"

"Yes, really," Mel said, tucking a golden tendril behind Court's ear. "You're perfect."

"I think you're perfect," Court answered. "And I love you."

Mel's heart skipped a beat. "You do?"

"Yes," Court said. She kissed her, pressed her body against Mel's and nudged her thigh between Mel's legs. A ripple of desire worked up her, threatening to obliterate her thoughts. But Court held her attention. She cupped Mel's face in one hand and said, "You don't have to say it back—I know this is fast. But I just want you to know how I feel."

"I love you too," Mel said. "It's not too fast for me."

Court beamed, then pounced on Mel. "You just made my day. And now I'm going to make yours."

She practically ripped Mel's underwear off, and pinned her to the bed as she made her intentions clear—it was her turn to take charge.

*C*ourt couldn't put off getting chewed out by her father forever.

After Court and Mel got out of bed and had a late breakfast in the apartment, lingering over their coffees, she knew she had to face him. She'd silenced her phone shortly after texting her dad just to let him know she was okay, but there were a handful of messages waiting for her.

One of which regarded her appointment with the precinct psychologist, set for the first available time today.

"I guess I should get down there," she said reluctantly around eleven-thirty. "My appointment is at one. That'll give my dad an hour and a half to yell at me for being irresponsible and impulsive."

"Do you still want me to come with?" Mel asked.

"No, you enjoy your day," Court said, kissing her forehead before she went to the dishwasher to load up her plate and mug. "I'll text you after my appointment, let you know how all of it went."

"I'm sure you'll do just fine—with your dad as well as the psychologist."

"Have you ever had to visit the shrink?" Court asked.

Mel shook her head. "Not the precinct psychologist. I did go to therapy after my mom left, though. Nonna found someone for me to talk things out with."

"Did it help?"

"Yeah. I mean, you never really get over being abandoned by your own mother," she said, "but now I know that it was her selfishness, not anything I did or was."

Court closed the distance between them in just a few seconds, throwing her arms around Mel so hard they ended up flopping onto the couch together. Court bearhugged her, squeezing her until she was convinced Mel knew how much she cared about her, then kissed her.

"I love you," she said. "I meant it when I said it last night. It wasn't just like, sex hormones or anything."

Mel smiled, wrapped her thighs around Court's legs. "I love you too. And now you're in trouble because I'm not sure I can let you get up off this couch."

They kissed some more, Mel's hand going beneath the T-shirt she'd loaned Courtney, cupping one breast and making her want to say to hell with her appointment and every other responsibility in the world.

But, alas, time didn't stand still when she was with Mel—it only felt that way sometimes. After a while, she managed to drag herself off the couch, pull Mel to her feet and kiss her once more in a safer standing position.

"Have a good day, babe."

"You too," Mel answered. "Remember, your dad only worries because he loves you."

Court was still thinking about those words... and the feeling of Mel's body wrapped around her own on the couch... when she got to her dad's office and knocked on the doorframe. He looked up from his desk, dark circles beginning to form under his eyes after pulling an all-nighter thanks to the Gilles case.

Court expected anger, or disappointment, or that stern dad look he'd perfected when she was in high school. Instead, he got up and was pulling Court into his arms in the blink of an eye.

"Dad–" she tried to object.

"Don't you 'Dad' me," he said, holding her tighter. "You had a gun pointed at you last night, and one of your colleagues got shot. I get to hug you in front of the whole damn precinct if I want to."

After a moment, he let go and she held up the bakery bag she'd brought with her. "I guess I don't need to sweeten you up with donuts, then?"

He took the bag. "Well, I am still mad at you for disobeying direct orders—as both my daughter and my employee." There was the stern dad look she'd been expecting. His voice was gruff as he said, "Come in and shut the door."

She did, sitting down in front of his desk while he resumed his own seat and opened the bakery bag. His eyes lit up when he saw the buttercream-filled donuts inside—the unhealthiest thing in the bakery, in Court's opinion—but she could tell he was trying not to look too eager as he pulled one out.

"Want one?" he asked.

Court waved him off. "I already had breakfast, thanks."

He arched a brow at her. This was pretty early in the day for a night-shift worker, and he knew her usual routine. She could see the gears working in his head, and he asked, "With Officer Pine?"

"Yes," Court said. "We've been seeing each other. I like her a lot."

Love, she thought... but it was probably too early to admit that to her dad.

"I like her too," he said, biting into his donut. "She's a good officer."

"I know," Court answered. Then she reached for a donut even though she really wasn't hungry. She just wanted something to stuff into her mouth after she admitted, "I've been thinking we might make good partners after I graduate the police academy."

She took a big bite, and her dad drew in a deep breath, getting ready to object. But then he deflated, taking the time to really think about what she said. Then he set down his donut and sat back in his chair. "The academy, huh?"

"I really want to be a police officer like you and Mom," Court said. Then, her heart pounding almost harder than it had been when she was standing in that little hunting cabin with Steven Larder, she said, "I'm going to take the civil service exam the next time it's offered, Dad. I don't care what you think about that—it's what I want and I can handle it."

"Yeah, I know you can," he said, and his words were nearly enough to knock Court right out of her chair.

"You do?"

"Look, I'm not about to condone what you did on the Gilles case, but after you got yourself into hot water, you handled yourself well," he said. "With proper training, you'll understand how to avoid dangerous situations before they develop."

"So... you're supporting this idea?"

He was giving her that stern look, but she could see in his eyes that he was warming up to it. "You're my daughter and I'll always think of you as my baby girl, but you're a grown woman who's perfectly capable of making her own decisions. You're also smart and compassionate and brave, and the force can always use more officers with those qualities."

Court was beaming by the time she walked out of her dad's office, and she sailed right through her psychologist appointment, getting released to go back to work right away.

*T*wo days later, she was just finishing up a dispatch shift—counting the days until the next civil service exam—when her cell rang and she saw Tom Logan's name on the screen.

"Hey, feeling better yet?" she answered as she logged out of her computer.

"Much," he said, and he sounded better too—far more alert than when she and Mel went to visit him in the ER.

"Get discharged yet?" she asked.

"The doc promised me it'll happen this afternoon," he said. "But before I leave, I've got business in the hospital. Steven Larder is finally stable enough to talk. You and Mel want to meet me, see what he has to say?"

"Absolutely," Court said. "I'll call her."

"Meet me in the post-op recovery ward in twenty," Tom said, and then he hung up.

Court met Mel in the precinct parking garage and they drove over to the hospital together. They found their way to post-op, and it didn't take much sleuthing to figure out which room belonged to Larder.

There was a cop stationed outside the door, just like O'Connell had been standing guard outside of Tom's room. But in this case, rather than protecting the occupant, the officer's job was to make sure Larder didn't try to make a run for it.

Mel flashed her badge and identified herself to the guard, and Court peeked through the window. "Larder's alone."

"Tom Logan been by here yet?" Mel asked the guard.

He was shaking his head just as the sound of rubber wheels squeaking on tile floors made everyone look up the hallway. Tom turned a corner in a wheelchair, wearing what seemed to be his work uniform—black, slightly wrinkled slacks with a white button-up shirt and a tie that had seen better days.

"There he is," the guard said, and Mel gave him a mildly sarcastic thanks.

They met Tom near the nurses' station and he asked, "How do I look? Not too intimidating, I hope?"

Court smiled. "You look great for a guy who got shot three days ago."

"Gee, thanks," he said. "Hey, Pine, I hear you took the lead interrogating Tucker."

"Yeah, Court and I told you that," Mel reminded him.

"Excuse me for not remembering," he said, putting a hand on his thigh where his pant leg was bulky from the bandages underneath. "I was a little distracted last time I saw you. Anyway, are you sure you don't wanna be a detective? Get off the streets?"

Mel looked to Court. They'd talked about the possibility of teaming up once Court graduated the police academy, and Court was already fantasizing about a *Rizzoli & Isles*-type TV show that would be inspired by their lives... but with a whole lot of blatantly sapphic overtones.

"Nah, I think I'm happy where I am," Mel told Tom.

"Fair enough," he nodded. "But do you wanna take the lead again one more time? I'm not sure I can play bad cop when I'm still down about a pint of blood."

"No problem," Mel said, and she led the way back to Larder's room.

The guard opened the door for them, then pulled it shut behind them. Steven Larder sat up the minute he saw that he had visitors. One arm was handcuffed to the thick plastic safety railing of the bed, and the chain clinked in protest as he adjusted his position.

"Why am I cuffed to this bed?" he demanded while Mel, Court and Tom arranged themselves in a semicircle around him, staying out of reach.

"Really, Mr. Larder?" Mel said, crossing her arms over her chest.

"Yeah, really," he shot back. "I gave you Adam Tucker. I told you I didn't do anything."

"You didn't steal a million dollars' worth of Iraqi gold and jewelry?" Tom asked.

"Well, fine... that," Larder said, trying to cross his own arms and finding himself unable. He settled for laying them awkwardly at his sides. "But that's not a police matter. How come there's a Fox County cop standing outside my door instead of an MP?"

"That's what we came here to talk to you about," Tom said, then nodded to Mel, handing the interrogation over to her.

She Mirandized Steven, then asked, "Did you kill Eric Gilles?"

"No," he said.

"But he was alive when he left the Tucker house," she said. "Rachel and Adam Tucker both swore to that."

"So?" Larder said. "How's that point to me?"

"You can thank your buddy Adam for that," Mel answered. "Turns out neither of you have any scruples about throwing each other under the bus at the first opportunity. He told us that he called you, that you drove Eric away from the Tucker house while Adam got his wife to the hospital. You were the last person to see Eric Gilles alive. So... tell us, Steven. What happened?"

Larder's hands turned to fists and he looked out the window. Fabricating an answer, or weighing his options? Court couldn't tell. They all just let him stew in silence for a minute or two, and then Tom said, "You're going away for a long time for all the things you stole. I bet it'd help your defense if Fox County can tell the court martial that you cooperated in our investigation."

Finally, Larder looked back at them. His gaze was steely as he locked eyes with Mel. If he wasn't hand-cuffed to the bed, Court would have stepped between them to protect her.

"Okay, look," he said. "Eric was a problem. He was going to mess everything up right when Tucker and I were about to cash in. Tucker called me to make sure he didn't cause any more trouble, so I came and got him."

"In his car?"

"It woulda been suspicious if his car stayed at Tucker's house," Larder said. "I parked a few blocks over and drove Eric's SUV."

"And where were you taking him?" Mel asked.

"To my house. I was going to keep him there for a week or two while Adam and I sold off all the jewelry," Larder said. "I had a buyer all lined up and it wouldn'ta taken that long—we were going to pass it off like he'd disappeared on a bender or something. He's done it before."

"And then what?"

"And then we'd let him go home!" Larder raised his voice. "The plan was never to kill him."

"But something went wrong," Mel said. "What?"

"He started shooting up while I was driving," Larder said. "I didn't know he had junk in the glovebox. I told him to cut it out but he was crying and talking about how he killed his sister. He thought she was dead and for all I knew, she was. I was just supposed to get him the hell away from Tucker's house. So I'm driving down the road and the crazy sonofabitch is sticking a needle in his arm, and the next thing I know he's slumped in the seat beside me and there's foam coming out of his mouth."

"You're saying he overdosed?" Tom asked.

"Yeah," Larder said. "I pulled over, I was freaking out. I didn't know what the hell to do."

"Did you attempt CPR?" Mel asked. "Did you consider, I don't know, calling the police?"

"Yeah, lady, that was at the top of my list—call the police to let them know my addict friend was ODing because he was upset that his sister was wearing the Iraqi jewelry we stole," he said, rolling his eyes. "I took his pulse—he didn't have one. It was too late."

"And then what?" Mel prompted.

"I panicked," Larder said. "Look, I'm not a killer."

"You shot me in the leg," Tom pointed out. "You easily could have killed me."

"I'm an expert marksman," Larder said. "If I wanted you dead, you wouldn't be sitting here now." Tom just gave him a hard stare, and Larder said, "Okay, okay, I'll admit to the fire. I lit the damn truck on fire because I never drove it before and I didn't want the cops to find my hair or some shit next to Eric's body. But I *did not* kill him."

"No, you just desecrated his corpse," Court said.

"Make no mistake about it, Mr. Larder," Tom said, wheeling a little closer so he could meet the man's eyes, "Eric Gilles would not be dead right now if it weren't for what you and Tucker did in Iraq. You can think that over while you wait for the MPs to conduct their own investigation."

With that, he spun his wheelchair around, letting it squeak so badly that Larder grimaced and his handcuff rattled again as he tried to reach up to cover his ears. Mel held the door for Tom, then she and Court followed him into the hallway.

"Wow..." she said once the door was closed. "So what happens next?"

"That's it," Tom answered. "At least for us. I write up my report, the Fox County prosecutor has his way with Larder and Tucker, and then we turn them over to the military police."

"I keep thinking about Rachel," Court said. "Lydia too, but Rachel lost her brother and now her husband is in jail, and she's still recovering from her head injury. That's a hell of a lot to go through."

"There is a little bit of a silver lining there," Tom said. "I got stir-crazy sitting in the hospital yesterday once I started to feel better, and figured it'd be a good time to cross some Ts, dot some Is. I made a few calls and found out that Eric's military pension is going to his estranged wife after all, but she's giving half of it to Rachel and Lydia."

"Well, that'll help with the medical bills, anyway," Court said.

"Sounds like they're mending fences," Mel added. "That's good. So, Court, your first official case is in the books."

"Not official," Tom interjected. "I'm in enough hot water with Wilson already. Let's not start throwing those kinds of words around."

Court chuckled. "Well, whatever it was, it feels good to be able to say 'case closed'."

A couple weeks after the police closed out their involvement in the Gilles case (and Larder and Tucker were awaiting their turn in front of both civil and military judges), Court convinced Mel to take a week off work.

"You haven't had a vacation since Zara left patrol, and I'm starting the police academy next week," she'd said one morning as they were climbing into bed after a long shift. "We can take the week, do whatever we want, go wherever we want. The world is our oyster."

Court had taken the civil service exam and passed with flying colors, as Mel knew she would. She had to admit that the prospect of spending long nights on patrol without Court in the dispatch office to keep her company wasn't something she was looking forward to.

"It *would* be nice to have you all to myself for a week before we're on different sleep schedules," Mel had agreed, and so that was how they ended up taking their first vacation together.

It had been somewhat spontaneous so they didn't have time to plan an actual trip, and Mel didn't want to be that far away from Nonna in case she needed her.

"You should go wherever you want, do whatever you want with that cute girl of yours," Nonna had told her when Mel let her know about their plans. "You're young —enjoy the freedom while you've got it."

"I can enjoy it right here at home," Mel had assured her.

The truth was that Nonna was actually doing much better lately. Her pneumonia had completely cleared up, and she was beginning to respond to the chemotherapy treatments in a really promising way. Even her oncologist was optimistic about how well she was doing for a seventy-two-year-old.

And so Mel had let Court talk her into taking a couple of day trips during their vacation.

They spent a day at Fox Lake beach, although the weather was turning cool and the wind coming off the water was chilly so they mostly huddled together on their beach blanket. It might have even been better than actually going into the water, spending the whole day with her head resting on Court's shoulder, her body curled up against her while Court read aloud from a lesbian romance novel that had some rather, ahem, *inspiring* scenes that they later played out back at Mel's apartment.

Another day, they drove out to the biggest outdoor flea market in the state and spent hours walking up and down the aisles, hunting for Degenhart glass and just enjoying the time together.

Court pointed out cute décor that she wanted to put in her first apartment when she moved out of her dad's house, and Mel realized that every time Court saw something new, Mel was imagining what it would look like in her own apartment.

They'd only been dating a short time. It was far too early to talk about moving in together... but then again, a lot of people would say it was too early to know that they loved each other. And those people would be wrong, because Mel knew that was true without a shadow of a doubt. Maybe they were just moving fast because they knew it was right, and they didn't want to waste any more time getting to the good part.

She was just opening her mouth to ask Court if moving in together was something she'd consider when Court's eyes went wide and she pointed to a stall full of glassware. "Look!"

"What?" Mel asked, and Court had her by the hand, dragging her across the aisle.

She pointed Mel to a little tray of Degenhart owls and asked, "Do you and Gloria need any of these?"

Mel tried not to get her hopes up too much. They were down to just a couple owls left to complete the collection, and naturally, they were the rarest ones. The odds of finding one on any given day at a flea market were pretty low, and most of the time she walked away empty handed.

She scanned over the owls. There were about two

dozen of them, a decent enough sample size, but most were pretty common–

"Oh my God!"

"What?" Court asked, excited already.

Mel picked up a dark-toned, opalescent owl with shades of blue, green and copper infused in the glass. She checked for the artist's mark on the base, and her heart actually started racing as she asked the stall owner, "Do you know which glass color this owl is?"

The woman pulled herself out of the collapsible lawn chair she'd been sitting in and came over, pasting on a smile as she sensed an impending sale. She lowered her eyeglasses from her forehead to the tip of her nose and inspected the owl Mel was holding.

"That there's the Carnival Cobalt," she said. "Pretty rare."

Yeah, I know, Mel thought... but it was haggling time so she kept a straight face. Court, on the other hand... she was beaming, squeezing Mel's arm and actually bouncing with excitement.

"You found one!" she said.

Mel tried to give her a *play it cool* look, but Court didn't pick up on it.

"How much do you want for it?" she asked the woman, who pondered the question like it was the most important thing in the world.

At last, she said, "Oh, I guess I could part with it for one-fifty."

"One hundred," Court chimed in.

The woman frowned, but Mel was already reaching

for her wallet. In truth, she would have paid more than one-fifty just to see the look on her grandmother's face when she finally got to hold a Carnival Cobalt owl in her hands. She'd have paid ten times that if Nonna had been well enough to actually come out to the flea market and find it herself.

In the end, they walked away with the glass owl wrapped delicately in bubble wrap, Mel's wallet a hundred and ten dollars lighter thanks to Court's negotiating. They linked arms and kept wandering the flea market, and Mel said, "In spite of your absolutely terrible poker face, one-ten is a good deal."

"Terrible poker face!" Court objected. "What are you talking about?"

"You lit up like a Christmas tree the minute that lady said 'Carnival Cobalt,'" Mel teased. "Something to work on when you get to the academy—you definitely can't let suspects read your face like that."

"Well, we got the owl and that's all that matters," Court said, head held high.

"Yeah, I've seen them going for over two hundred online," Mel admitted. "I would have gone higher. It is kinda crazy that we just happened to find one of the rarest Degenharts when we came out here on a whim."

"Uh, yeah," Court said, then spotted a stall selling homemade caramel corn up ahead. "Ooh, snack time?"

She started to pull Mel toward the food, but Mel had a lot of years of police experience and she knew when someone was trying to distract her. She stopped short, right there in the middle of the aisle, and when Court's forward momentum was arrested, she spun around to face her.

"What?"

"*Was* it a whim?" she asked, narrowing her eyes to study Court's face. She didn't have to try too hard— Court's cheeks colored immediately and she looked sheepish. "Court!"

"Okay, you got me," she said. "I called around a little bit. That's not cheating, is it?"

Mel wasn't actually sure where Nonna would stand on that subject... but she knew where *she* stood. She wrapped both arms around Court's neck, planting a long, deep, appreciative kiss on her lips. The crowds parted as foot traffic flowed around them, and a few people gawked as they passed, but Mel and Court were oblivious, entirely in a world of their own.

When she pulled back, Mel left her nose brushing against Court's and she looked into those deep, gorgeous eyes as she said, "It's not cheating... it's the nicest thing anyone's ever done for me."

Then she kissed her again. She never wanted to stop kissing her. In this moment, and for the rest of her life.

EPILOGUE 2
CLARK

*H*e sat in his car, the engine idling and the headlights turned off so as not to attract attention to himself. He was parked at the end of a row of units at UStore Self-Storage, just before the turn for the unit he'd rented.

He'd been coming out here every couple of days for weeks with no problem. He'd scoped the place out ahead of time, and it had seemed ideal. Lots of units, outdoors and without any security cameras. He had to punch in a code at the entrance to open the gate, but there was never anybody here who cared about who came and went.

Best of all, the whole place was pretty run-down, and Clark had never actually seen another renter, or an employee.

He hadn't thought he'd need his unit forever—just a month or two until his new friend stopped fighting him and came to understand that he wanted what was best for her. Then she could come and live with him in his apartment instead of the storage unit.

The one he was looking at now, with police tape crisscrossed over the door.

His heart had stopped in his chest as soon as he saw it, and his first instinct was to gun the accelerator, get the hell out of there. Obviously, something had gone horribly wrong with Jenny, and he didn't need to get out of his car and open the storage unit to know that she was gone.

But flooring it, peeling out of there like a maniac, wasn't going to do him any favors. What he needed now was to keep a low profile, just like he had after Belle and AJ died.

Damn it.

He pounded on the steering wheel with one fist. This was those two all over again. All he'd wanted was to be their friend, and they never appreciated him. They avoided him and they mistreated him, and when he went over to their apartment to find out why, they'd acted like he was a monster.

Now they were both dead, and Jenny might be too. That, or sitting in a police station right this minute telling the cops what he looked like, how they'd met, no doubt lying through her teeth about what a bad guy he was.

He'd treated her well, hadn't he? Sure, nobody *wants* to live in a storage unit, but it wasn't going to be forever, and he'd visited as often as he thought was safe. Brought her whatever food she wanted. Reading material. Even drugs, which had been scary as hell to acquire.

He could have helped her get off that stuff. She could

have lived a better life if she had just opened her eyes and seen what he was trying to do for her.

Clark found that he was white-knuckling the steering wheel and he forced himself to loosen his grip. Then he forced himself to get out of the car and see what he could find out inside the storage unit. It didn't matter now—they knew his face, his car... he'd have to ditch his Eddie Banks alias. That was trash now, but it was easy enough to get a new name.

A new friend, on the other hand... those weren't nearly as easy to come by.

Jenny'd had promise. He'd known that since they first met. Too bad it had to turn out this way... again.

He went quickly over to the storage unit, sticking close to the walls just in case UStore had installed more cameras since the cops had last been here. He pulled his sleeve down over his hand and used it to rip the police tape off the door. His lock was long gone. He pulled the roll door up and grimaced at the stale, pungent smell within. Old fast food mixed with the smell of human waste—that was unavoidable, though he'd tried to keep the place as clean as he could for Jenny.

But now there was a new smell. Something ripe and sweet-sour, which made bile rise in the back of his throat. He'd never smelled a decomposed corpse before, but if he had to guess, that's what he would put his money on.

The unit was empty now, with no sign other than that smell to clue him in on what had happened here. Clark was a smart guy, though. He could fill in the blanks for himself, and he walked away from the unit satisfied that Jenny was dead, not telling the cops about him.

He left the police tape where it had fallen and walked briskly back to his car. That was trash now, just like Eddie Banks, but there were a lot of places around this city where you could leave a car unlocked and come back an hour later to find it gone.

He'd get a new car, a new name.

And then he'd find himself a new friend.

A NOTE FROM CARA

Hello!

Thank you so much for reading *Radio Silence* – I hope you enjoyed it!

If you'd like to be notified when I publish a new book, sign up to my newsletter at https://bit.ly/2LPRHXI - I send out a monthly email packed with **free short stories, behind-the-scenes details into my works in progress and all kinds of fun stuff.**

You can also connect with me on social media using the icons below.

With love,

Cara

 facebook.com/caramalonebooks

twitter.com/caramalonebooks

goodreads.com/caramalonebooks

bookbub.com/authors/cara-malone

It was a dark and stormy morning...

That was the thought that blew through Dr. Amelia Trace's mind the minute she stepped out of her condo and the wind whipped her blonde hair over her face. It stuck to her tinted lip balm and tangled around the chunky tortoise shell frames of her glasses, and there it would have to stay until she got to her car because she had a lunch bag and briefcase in one hand and a steaming travel mug of coffee in the other.

The skies were eerily dark even though it was only a little past seven-thirty in the morning. Daylight savings time had begun a few weeks ago, so her morning commute was no longer pitch-black—at least on an ordinary day.

This morning, a serious storm was brewing and Amelia just hoped she would get to the office before the skies opened up and all those heavy rain clouds dumped their contents on her. She got to her BMW parked in the driveway and a struggle ensued between her, the door, and the wind. It damn near made off with her coffee mug, but in the end, Amelia prevailed.

She needed that coffee—it was a Monday morning and those tended to be the busiest of the week. She was the chief medical examiner for the county, and her first task of the week was always to check on the cases that had come in over the weekend. Then she would distribute them among herself and the other four pathologists in the office.

If anything happened over the weekend that wouldn't keep until Monday, whoever was on call would have to come in and work, and this weekend it had been Amelia's turn. Of course, with her luck, that meant she'd spent all day Sunday in the morgue working on an apparent homicide victim that had been badly decomposed.

Hence the mug of extra-strong coffee this morning.

On her twenty-minute drive to the office, the mug stayed in its cupholder and Amelia drove with both hands clamped to the wheel as the wind buffeted her car and threatened to shove her out of her lane. It had been a pretty rainy spring so far, but this weather was something else and by the time Amelia pulled into the ME's lot, she was stressed and shaken by the drive. She parked, then sat in the car for a minute, regaining her composure and sipping her coffee in peace before the day began.

"Oh, that's the good stuff," she said, closing her eyes to really savor the creamy hazelnut blend.

She'd allowed her sister Frances to talk her into buying a fancy Nespresso coffee maker a few weeks ago. Even though she knew Frannie mostly wanted it for when she came to visit, Amelia couldn't deny the appeal now that she had it.

But the wind just kept rocking her car, refusing to let her forget that at any moment a torrential downpour could unleash itself. "Okay, let's do this," she said, gathering her things. She pushed her door open, again with significant resistance, and the wind whipped it shut as soon as she was clear. *Bang.*

And then, nothing.

In an instant, the wind died, the world fell silent, and the hairs on the back of Amelia's neck stood on end.

"Oh shit," she said, seconds before a siren began to wail in the distance. Amelia took off at a run across the parking lot. She lost her grip on her mug—as well as her lunch bag—and left them both where they fell. She reached the medical examiner's office and burst through the door, shouting to her wide-eyed receptionist, "Tornado—get to the basement!"

"Seriously?" the girl, Reese, asked.

Amelia nodded. "Seriously. Go!"

This wasn't the first time in her ten years here that the tornado siren had gone off and she and her staff had to take cover, but it was the first time she'd actually been standing outside and felt the wind die, felt the air crackle with electricity. It felt real, imminent. And it scared the hell out of her.

Fortunately, Reese didn't need telling twice. She got up and bolted through the lobby, heading for the basement, and Amelia called after her, "Take the stairs, not the elevator."

Amelia didn't follow her. As the boss, it was her responsibility to make sure all her employees were safe, even though her pulse was racing so fast she was damn near palpitations. She made a quick circuit through the investigators' cubicles, getting them all to take the siren seriously, and thankfully everyone on the administrative side of the building had already been sufficiently spooked to go downstairs.

Reese must have warned Dylan and Elise, the lab techs, on her way to the basement because their labs were empty. Amelia made sure the morgue was too—at least empty of those with a pulse.

The siren became muted the deeper into the building

Amelia went, but she could hear the wind picking up again, reaching a train whistle pitch as she got to the stairwell. Oh God, she thought as she practically flew down the stairs, that's exactly what they say tornados sound like right before they touch down.

"Amelia, in here!" somebody called to her the second her feet touched the concrete floor. A hand hooked around her elbow and her lead investigator, Maya, was pulling her into the women's locker room.

"Is everyone accounted for?" she asked as they rushed past a small row of metal lockers and into the tiled shower area.

"Best we can figure," Maya said. "It's time for a shift change so everybody we know was in the building is down here."

That would just have to be good enough, because in that moment, the overhead lights died and somebody—Reese, maybe?—let out a yelp. Amelia's ears popped as the air pressure spiked, and she crouched in the dark, feeling along the cool tile floor until she found the wall. Then a coworker clutched her hand.

"Hold on, everybody," Amelia said. "It'll be okay."

Ironic words for a woman who dealt with death day in and day out, and investigated cases where people were very much not okay. *It'll be okay* wasn't a promise anyone could actually make.

But sometimes platitudes were all you had to hold on to—that and an anonymous coworker's hand.

Continue reading

Calling all lesfic lovers!

Join us for a monthly book club, talk to your favorite lesfic authors, check out our growing community of published and aspiring writers, and hang out in daily chats with fellow lesfic lovers. Check out the group at http://tinyurl.com/lesficlove

Printed in Great Britain
by Amazon

63321378R00139